Calculation

Aquarius

Maggie Jane Schuler
&
Morgan Heyward

Copyright

Copyright © 2020 Maggie Jane Schuler & Morgan Heyward
All rights reserved
This book is protected under the copyright laws of the U.S. Copyright Act of 1976. No part of this book may be reproduced in any form or by any electronic or mechanical means, including information storage and retrieval systems, without written permission from the author, except for the use of brief quotations in a book review or blog. Scanning, uploading, and electronic sharing of this book without the permission of the publisher or author constitutes unlawful piracy and theft.

This is a work of fiction. Names, characters, places, events, media, trademarked brands, businesses, and/or organizations are the product of the author's imagination or are used fictitiously. Any resemblance to actual persons, living or dead, events, or locales is entirely coincidental.

Editing: Amy Senethavilay
Beloved Ink Editors and Proofing

Print ISBN: 978-1-7342145-5-0

Dedication

For all those who believe they can do it all alone in this crazy world and come to realize it's alright to depend on others.

As the Beatles noted, "I get by with a little help from my friends!"

Calculation

AQUARIUS

JANUARY 21ST – FEBRUARY 20TH

AQUARIUS

Chapter One

Caelum

"That's it, baby. Yes, right there."

My hands tunneled under the ridiculous amount of material decorating the ass of my latest conquest. Why women covered their bodies in yards of the stuff, stumped me. Didn't they realize less was more? Right now, the silky material decorated my prize like a Twinkie—its layers flipped up and over her back, exposing the coveted filling every kid desired from their cake covered treat.

I slid a hand between us and strummed her clit as she ground the heart-shaped ass that attracted me in the first place, against the abs I worked like a mother for in the gym. Finding her panty less made our little tête-à-tête in the maintenance closet of the reception hall much more convenient.

Her breaths burst forth in short pants of 'oh's and yeah's' with an 'oh my god' or three thrown in as I worked her into a frenzy. The pace of my fingers and hips destined to launch her like a rocket in less time than a NASA countdown, if the flutters squeezing me were any indication.

A *thud* against the door quickened my pace, and I hammered into her, sure to set her off into the stratosphere at any moment.

"I swear to God, Caelum, if you're locked in this closet..."

I grinned, gave her a little prodding pinch, then covered her moan with my other hand. *Liftoff.* She clenched around me like a vice, and I gave up the fight immediately after with a satisfied grunt of my own. She jerked then turned her head as my finger slid from her sensitive nub. The evidence of her pleasure glossed my lips as I gave her the shush sign and motioned toward the door. Panic laced her brown eyes as I cocked an ear and kept the finger planted against my lips. A reminder we were on a mission of secrecy. I'm really a Class A bastard when all is said and done.

A rapid-fire *bang, bang, bang* pounded on the door as the handle jiggled where I locked it a short time ago. Experience taught me to expect the unexpected, and contingency plans were necessary for all aspects of my profession and personal life. Case in point: the jiggling lock and my friend's exasperated voice on the other side.

"Come with me," along with moving shadows, slipped under the door. I glanced at the single light swinging from the ceiling, paying homage to the man above who saved my ass from facing the bride and groom at this moment.

Calculation

I knew that after I gave this sweet treat before me a wink and nod at the altar, I'd be peeling off her wrap of a dress between the reception line and my Best Man's speech. Yes, I was *that* kind of an asshole. Ride 'em hard and put 'em away wet. In this case, responsibility tugged at my conscience before I dove in. Every single man alive knew weddings brought out the vipers. Their hooked fangs puncturing your freedom and poisoning your future as only a single woman could do.

My father warned me about doing the right thing when my hormones flared and I started dating. I prided myself on the fact that not once did a woman enrapture me so thoroughly that I forgot protection. With a twist of my hips, I slipped from the wedding present to myself and gave her a smack on the ass that had her standing ramrod straight with a startled "Hey."

A crooked smile decorated my face as I tossed the condom in a trashcan to my left. "We need to get going. I have a speech to give."

Her gaze followed my work-roughened hands as I tucked my shirt back into the tuxedo pants and zipped up. She wasn't the only one in the bridal party without panty lines. I found commando a benefit to these situations and made good use of that when I went out on the town. Or, my best friend's wedding, in this instance.

I grabbed my jacket and shrugged it on as Twinkie girl unrolled her skirt and smoothed the wrinkles.

"Will I see you again?"

Yeah, not so much.

"Of course you will. In about…" I checked my watch and frowned. "…five minutes if we don't get our asses moving."

I unlocked the door and gave a swivel of my head both ways. With a mumbled "Thanks," and no kiss, a rule I lived and died by, I rushed off down the hall toward the ballroom where I knew my best friend waited to rip me a new asshole as he smiled at his new bride. Was it worth it? I straightened my bow tie and slid sticky fingers through my hair in an attempt to mask my rumpled appearance. Hell yeah, it was. Any piece of ass, especially the cream filled morsel from the closet, was worth it. Now, if my buddy asked me if it was meaningful…

That was a question best left unanswered.

The reception hall echoed with the chatter of voices and utensils on plates as guests dined on their catered dinner in groups of eight. As I approached the head table, my

Calculation

friend glared and motioned me closer to his chair.

"You are fucking lucky that door was locked." His hissed enunciation on each individual syllable.

My cocky grin slipped a little as my best friend, Jordan, seethed with frustration at my recklessness. Typical playboy behavior he'd told me before, and I embodied the image. I held a microphone in one hand and a glass of champagne in the other, prepared to address the crowd with my ad-libbed speech. He grabbed my jacket and jerked me backward as I leaned in to kiss Bartlett on the cheek.

"This is Bart's day. Don't fuck it up, man. I mean it."

A trickle of regret slid down my spine as the woman of the hour smiled up at me with a giddy glow that only appears with pure happiness.

She and Jordan met in college. One of those love stories that made you gag and thankful you're single in the same breath. I shivered as I straightened back up and put on my best panty-dropping grin. *No way in hell* would that happen to me. True love was for suckers. I didn't fit into that mold. I liked my freedom.

Feedback squealed over the amplifier as I flipped the microphone on. All eyes focused on me as I straightened my six and a half foot frame. I scanned the audience like the leader I was and scoped out the interested looks guaranteeing me some additional extracurricular activity later that evening. My eyes twinkled as I grinned further into the crowd and cleared my throat.

"Today was a great day…"

"Captain. Groupie at your six."

Our newest engineer frowned and nodded at the doorway as the Twinkie girl from my pre-reception tryst entered the station with a platter of cookies.

"Remind me later to kick Jordan's ass," I mumbled and stood from the table where my crew sat for our shift briefing. If this was payback for messing around at Jordan's wedding, I wanted assurance from my friend the debt was paid. The woman knew Bartlett from her college days, and Jordan graciously gave her my work address when she asked about me. *Asshole.*

"Hey, Candace." My crew gave her a small wave from the table as I ground my teeth. The woman stopped by every shift bearing gifts for the last three weeks. Don't get me wrong, we all loved dessert, but her constant veiled innuendos disrupted our workplace. My chief witnessed her visit last shift with a frown of his own after she

Calculation

grabbed my ass when she thought no one was looking.

"Knock that shit off, Captain. This is neither the time or the place." He'd taken me aside and laid down the law. Either I get my crap together, or he'd do it for me while I was on administrative leave.

I intercepted her at the doorway and turned her back around and out into the truck bay. "We are in the middle of a meeting, then leaving for training in about ten minutes."

She leaned close and rubbed her breasts against my chest as she balanced her tray. "I told you to call me Candy."

With a sigh, I pushed her back and shook my head. "Candace, after your antics last shift, I've been told you are no longer welcome at the station." She didn't need to know I was throwing my chief under the bus. Let him be the bad guy.

"Why?" Her tray slid to the bumper of the engine with a crash as she crossed her arms. "What about us?"

Fuck. This is why I hated wedding hook-ups. Why I chose one and done. Why I didn't share my phone number or work number. *Expectations*. Women read into things. Sex meant emotion to them. Sex meant relationship. Neither of those things fit into my single life goals. "Candace, we had sex. That's it. There is no us."

I stepped back as she screeched in dismay. "You led me on. You lying piece of shit. How can you say there is no us?"

My hands popped up in the universal sign of 'Whoa' as I stepped back another few inches from the rapidly spiraling situation. I never intended to see her again after the wedding. Jordan instigated this confrontation. "Candace, you need to leave. I'm sorry you misinterpreted our hook-up. It was enjoyable, but that's all it was."

"You bastard."

The slap of her hand across my face caught me off guard. I stood in place watching her exit the bay, the tap of her shoes the only other sound besides the snickers of laughter from inside the station. A package of frozen peas landed in my hand as Ethan stood next to me and followed my gaze. My engineer and the new kid to the crew, he had only been on the job for three years. Quite mature for his young age, I expected the sage wisdom he spilled with his next breath.

"Dodged a bullet there, Cap."

I nodded in agreement, amazed I didn't pick up on her psychotic stalker nature before now. "Yeah. You got that right."

"I think you should call Jordan. Before this comes back and bites you in the ass."

I nodded once more. The last thing I needed was Jordan *and* Bart calling me out before I gave my side of the story. "Yeah, me too."

"Glad we had this talk, Cap."

He clapped me on the back as I stared at the car zooming out of the parking lot in a cloud of burned rubber. I placed the peas against my burning cheek with a frown. A tingle, or perhaps a shiver from the frozen bag on my skin, crawled along my spine and raised the hairs at my nape. Somehow, somewhere, I knew karma smiled and rubbed their hands together in glee. *Waiting.*

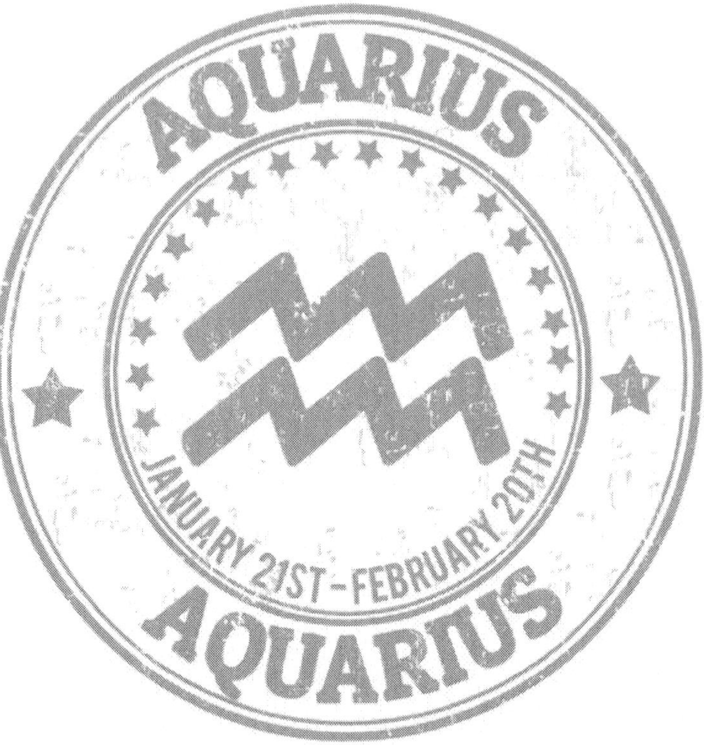
AQUARIUS
JANUARY 21ST - FEBRUARY 20TH
AQUARIUS

Chapter Two

Ximena

The minty smell of paste coated the air as the chatter of little mouths rose to a crescendo of high pitched squeals and giggles. The delightful melody of *The Nutcracker* played in vain; classical music—intended to calm the little balls of energy, washed away as the preschoolers finished gluing googly eyes to their handprints turned reindeer; all in the name of holiday cheer. *Bah humbug* rolled through my mind.

"You doing alright?" Lorna, the director of the school, laid her hand on my shoulder.

"Of course." My chin quivered, telling more of the truth than the lie which slipped between my lips and the halfhearted lift of my head.

"I know this is tough, but she's going to be fine."

"Mm-hmm," hummed from deep in my throat as my eyes perused the fifteen three-year-olds now eating the paste and digging their pudgy fingers in the jars rather than gluing down the red puff balls for Rudolph's nose.

"I promise, she's too strong not to pull through."

"Whoa, Trevor, let's not stick the glue in our nose." I knelt down to help the wayward boy before a tear slipped through my guard. My goal today, set before walking in the door, focused on making it through the Christmas pageant and waving the last student goodbye until January. Three weeks of relaxation beckoning me with each tick of the hands of time.

Lorna greeted the parents and gathered the toddlers to the carpet, allowing me the time to gather my thoughts after her statement sat ignored but ingested.

"Good morning, boys and girls."

My threes all crooned with excitement in a choral response, "Good morning, Ms. Webster." Lorna loved these kids like her own. I'm not sure how when they wiped their noses on one another and refused to wash properly after the restroom.

"Are we all ready to show our moms and dads how we celebrate the season here at Shepherds of the Cloth?"

"Yes, Ms. Webster." My parent helpers moved toward the exit, thankful they listened to the director before I walked my class over to the dressing room behind the pulpit.

With a final cleansing breath, I nodded at Lorna and slid next to her. "Can we wave goodbye to Ms. Webster and our mommies and daddies while we meet with the other classes and get our costumes?"

Calculation

The energy sitting on the floor before me buzzed with excitement as they all turned and waived to the parent helpers. Lorna escorted the adults to the sanctuary without a hitch. "Ninety minutes," I repeated as we lined up and moved to the backstage area with the other six classes.

※

"Cheers!" Glasses clinked together from four of my colleagues as we sat in the bar off the beaten path of town. If the parishioners knew how much we celebrated after their cherubs went home, we'd probably all be prayed for with a suggestion we go to rehab.

"How is she?" Shelley whispered as the others flirted with the bartender while awaiting their drinks.

"She's gonna pull through. I'll know more tomorrow morning."

"Where's Charles?"

I chuckled at his name. "Chuck is off saving the financial markets until next Tuesday."

"Oh. At a time like this he—"

My hand held high stopped her. "He's not a fan of illness or responsibility." I lifted my frosty glass and took a long pull of my Sea Breeze. More vodka than cranberry—the way I liked it.

"You've been seeing one another since what, tenth grade?"

"Seems that way." I gulped the last of my drink and signaled the girls for another.

"Perfect."

"That's like saying fine, only you've got a little more snark attached."

I smirked as Julie and Melody waltzed back; a little noodle-kneed and unaware of the trail of eyes attached to their asses.

If only these men knew how wrong they were about those two. Heck, if Shepherds of the Cloth knew, they'd probably release them too.

For many reasons, we always chose to drink out of our city limits. Most often, we frequented a little pub in Portland, Eye of the Tiger. Every hour, piped-in music played the refrain from the song that made Survivor famous during the big build-up in the film *Rocky*. The college folks—not that we were that far out of college in our mid-twenties— loved the bar, and we were camouflaged among them.

Tonight's crowd hummed a different tune. Less college kids and more—

"Holy shit!" Shelley gripped my forearm tight below the table.

Julie and Melody turned in time as five of the most physically fit, model gorgeous men sauntered through the door. Not one of them in the final blooming stages of boy to manhood. They were all broad shoulders, chiseled jawlines, pecks which stood out under their Henley's, and the one who passed our table first had glutes that made his jeans weep just holstering each perfect globe.

"Well, this just got interesting." Melody gulped her margarita as the lights dimmed in the bar.

"I think that's my cue to call a taxi and head out."

"You're staying at El Conquistador, right? It's five minutes away. You're not leaving us early to go sit alone. You already told us Chuck is out of town until Tuesday." Julie unfolded her hand from Melody's and pointed at me.

Shelley nodded in agreement with Julie and added, "Why? You afraid you might like what you see and realize Charles is not right for you?"

"I know better than to stay at the bar once the crowds start arriving. It tells me I've already had too much to drink, and something good must be on the television by now besides the news."

"Stop living under a rock. We have the whole weekend here in Portland. And look at those muscles upon muscles." Shelley's hand waved the waitress our direction.

"Come on, Ximena, if Julie and I can hang here and make it through hetero land, why can't you? You can stay and be Shelley's wingman?"

I sighed, "Chuck might be out of town, but I'm not a cheater. The men who walked in look like trouble."

"Trouble for your kitty!" Shelley threw her head back with a squeal as the waitress found her way to our table.

We all placed our orders—mine a glass of water. One of us needed a sound mind. The crowd continued to build, and the noticeable difference showed in the lack of college kids tonight. It never dawned on me the college kids would be gone for the holiday, too.

Melody leaned in close, her speech a little slurred, "Why would you chink you might sheet on Chuck?" Julie giggled next to her but stared at me like a puppy waiting for a treat.

"I did not say I would cheat on Chuck."

"I bet if you call Charles right now, he'll tell you he's out with his colleagues." Shelley air quoted colleagues. "And I'll bet he's out with his one colleague, Janice, who's been his travel companion the last year. The one who snubbed you at the few events he asked you to the year prior."

"Look, I haven't asked him for more. I'm busy trying to figure out if preschool is my calling. I want to go to grad school or travel or—"

Together Julie and Melody chimed out, "Not commit to Charles and Janice to be in a ménage?"

"Ugh. You guys are impossible." I pushed back from the table with a sigh, then wedged my way through the crowd to the restroom. I love these ladies, but they've been relentless about Chuck since New Year's Eve last year. He's not a bad guy, but our lives followed two different paths. He's all money—all high-roller mumbo jumbo. I'm covered in snot and tears and sneezes, trying to figure out if I'm cut out to coddle toddlers and build self-esteem in young minds. I clicked the lock on the stall and continued to think about my plight. One where I realized Chuck and Janice do travel a lot, and she usually does snub me and ignore me when I stop by his office. I zipped up my jeans, knowing what I needed to do and figuring it was high time I do it.

The warmth of water stuck to my hands and never crept into my frozen heart. I shut Charles out a long time ago, and why we continued playing happy couple was beyond me. The mirror reflected a tired me. The heavy bags under my eyes decided it might be best to get back to the hotel, make that phone call, and settle this before the holidays. Before I had to sit down on Christmas day for brunch with his mother, who only spoke about the old wealth my family continued to grow as the vineyards they owned prospered worldwide. She loved the idea of Charles marrying into my family for money that wasn't mine. She cared less if we actually loved one another.

The squeak of the door caught my attention.

"You alright?" Shelley stood still waiting for my answer.

"Yep. I know it's time."

"I've known you for too long, and he makes you complacent, not vibrant. You need someone who makes you glow."

"Well, then let's go dance a little before I make that call." I laced my arm with hers as we made our way back to the table. My shoulders felt a bit lighter, knowing I'd free myself of this lie very soon. However, it sucked to think of spending the holidays answering questions from my mother about why Charles didn't make me happy. She questioned me months ago, and I fed her so much bullshit I think her waders overflowed. To admit to her she knew before me that we were not a good match seemed a moot point.

Julie and Melody danced on the parquet floor to Michael Jackson's *Beat It* as we exited the hallway to the bathroom. All the men in the bar watched as they danced in sync and enjoyed themselves without judgment.

"Would you like to dance?" A warm hand tapped my shoulder.

Shelley attempted to unfold her arm from mine, but I pulled her back too quickly. "We're getting ready to meet our friends out on the floor. But thank you."

"It looks like they're doing just fine."

With a shrug of my shoulder, I brushed off his hand and drug Shelley to the dance floor. We found ourselves a small space next to Julie and Melody and joined them.

"He's watching you." Her hand poked a line right through me. I knew the man who entered with his entourage of hotties earlier, followed Shelley and me from the back of the bar. His stare burned holes through my jeans as the girls and I shook our money makers over the last two songs. His palm on my shoulder sent my nerves into hyperdrive. A sensation I lost somewhere between prom and college with Charles.

"He's just watching a show of four women body grinding one another. Men like that sort of fantasy."

Shelley's cheeks flushed even under the disco lights. "I don't think you know my fantasy." The words came from the heated body suddenly invading my personal space from behind.

Oh, shit. My eyes plead with Shelley's, but she turned and made a threesome with our friends. *Traitor.*

"I'm pretty sure I know exactly your type." My feet shuffled a turn. A feeble attempt at trying to distance myself from the well-built stranger. He gripped my waist and fawned up and down my body with the beat of the music.

"Go get it, Cap," screamed from across the floor.

"Tell me about my type over a drink." He grabbed my hand, pulling me off the dance floor.

A glance over my shoulder only left me frustrated as the girls blew me a kiss and waved me into the arms of the stranger, ignoring my wishes. He stopped and whispered into the ear of the waitress before seating us at a booth in the far dark corner.

"Let's make this painless." He rubbed circles with his thumb on the back of my hand.

"I think you're making this something it is not."

"How so?" Two tumblers slid across the table, and the waitress left without a word.

"I don't drink." My fingers pushed the glass to the edge of the table.

"Really?" His brow raised as he took the glass and downed the caramel colored liquid.

"What is that?"

"Coke."

"Coke?"

"Yeah. A classic. I like classic things. Go ahead, try yours."

Calculation

He pushed the glass back in my direction. With hesitation, I leaned in and sniffed the liquid. "Coke."

"Yep. I rarely drink. I've seen too many bad things happen when people drink too much."

"Hmm." I left the Coke alone. Not because I didn't love a good swig of the bubbly goodness, but out of principle. Who knows what the waitress slipped in it.

"So, you new in town or just here for the holidays?" He nodded to the untouched glass asking for permission.

"Your Coke. Here for—" I hesitated. His big, blues caught me off guard. With a five o'clock shadow masking his bold jawline, and the thick, dirty blond haircut high and tight, those broad shoulders turned toward me in full attention of what I might utter to him, something about him spoke secretly to my heart. A heart I thought would be broken tonight as I dreaded the phone call back East. The answer from a hotel room I had a feeling wasn't being singularly occupied and hadn't been singularly occupied for a long time. "God, how could I be so stupid." My hands found residence upon my forehead; I shook from head to toe out of frustration and anger at myself.

"Tell me what you're doing here. I can make things disappear." The final empty suction from the straw in my previously offered glass slurped with the last drops of the Coke.

My head lifted with my stifled chuckle at the pun.

"I like it when you laugh. It's what caught my eye when you were taking a shot back there at the table with your friends."

"I did not take a shot." My brain thought back to when the group of handsome men walked into the bar. "How about you? What's your story?" I tilted my head at his friends as they whistled and cheered him on from across the bar.

"I've been here on my days off helping my buddy fix and clean stuff up. They had a grease fire a few weeks ago. I take it you didn't know this was the first night he's been open since the fire?"

"Interesting."

"Perhaps."

"I need to go." I scooted across the vinyl cushion and settled my small clutch back across my chest.

"Tomorrow?"

"Maybe."

He grinned, and the dimples highlighted the glint in his eye. "Seven. I'll get us a table."

"Where?"

"Tell me where to pick you up?"

"Here."

With that, I waved across the dance floor to where Shelley found a dance

Calculation

partner, and the girls danced with everyone in some sort of line dance I'm far too uncoordinated and impatient to learn.

The cool night air tingled as it hit the heat of my hot cheeks. The phone call never placed for a taxi. I dreaded the short walk back to the hotel, but tonight gave me a reason to dial that final goodbye.

AQUARIUS

JANUARY 21ST – FEBRUARY 20TH

AQUARIUS

Chapter Three

Caelum

A huge neon sign in the shape of a Bengal tiger blazed in red and orange over the pub entrance. Customers filed inside in waves, happy once again that their regular watering hole opened back up for business. My buddy, Brad, pulled out all the stops tonight, and my crew and I promised a show of solidarity after the work we put into fixing the place up. A grand re-opening of sorts after a fire destroyed the kitchen and a good portion of the antique tin covering the ceiling last month. The memories of that morning flashed with the hum of the neon sign as I reached the doors.

"This is Cal." I cracked a bleary eye and squinted at the clock beside my bed. The panicked voice of my friend Brad on the other end jolted further thoughts of sleep from my body.

"Caelum, it's destroyed."

"Wait. What?" I sat up and flicked the bedside light on. My department pager laid on the floor at my feet. As I picked it up, it vibrated and showed three missed pages. Ah, shit. "What's destroyed?" The familiar screech of air brakes on Brad's end had me up and pulling on clothes in seconds.

"There was a fire at The Eye. It's a nightmare, man. I think everything's gone. It's only been three years. Fuck! What am I going to do?"

I grabbed my keys and some gum from my dresser as I shrugged on a jacket. "Listen, I'm on my way. I'll talk to the investigator on scene, and we can go from there."

"Okay."

His defeated sigh slammed me right in the gut. He worked hard to get the bar up and running. Unfortunately, if the fire started in the grease trap I told him to get cleaned months and months ago, his insurance might not cover all of the repairs. "I'll be there in twenty minutes or so. Hang tight, buddy. We'll work through this."

Once I spoke to the investigator, I knew Brad was up shit creek. The initial walkthrough assessment confirmed my fears. Instead of the "I told you so" routine, I volunteered my licensed carpenter and restoration services like the great friend I was and harangued the rest of my crew into providing free labor for free drinks and all the hot chicks they could handle.

"Cap. Twelve o'clock."

An elbow nudged my ribs, and I looked over at a smirking Ethan. His gaze focused on a table six feet in front of us filled with a multitude of empty glasses and beautiful

Calculation

single women, based on their ringless fingers. I kept up the pace and grinned at the gasp of "Holy shit," as I passed by. We worked out and kept our bodies in tip-top shape. Mandatory in our line of work when lives depended on us and the strength of our muscles. Ethan nudged me again and nodded at the strobe lights flashing over the crowd. Brad came through on his promise. The tight little bodies in barely-there dresses on the dance floor were ripe for the picking, and we had front row seats. *Oh, yeah.*

"Hello, my friend. Glad to see you." Brad gripped my hand in a solid shake as his bartender flipped bottlecaps from frosty beers and slid them across the polished wood bartop to the guys. A sarsaparilla stopped in front of me. Packaged in a frosty brown bottle, the carbonated soda quenched my thirst without the added alcohol. I only partook on special occasions. Never when I was behind the wheel.

"Thanks for coming tonight, guys. This wouldn't have been possible without the help of all of you." Brad shook everyone's hands, his gleaming eyes filled with gratitude. "I'm in your debt."

His words melted into The B-52's song playing in the background, so I leaned in close. "You know better than to offer an open promise to a bunch of firemen."

Brad's sheepish smile and wink caught me off guard. I raised an eyebrow and waited for the proverbial shoe to drop. "Tell you what. Pick any woman in here, and I'll get you their name and number before you leave. How's that?"

I knew a sucker bet when I heard one. He kept the carbon copies of every credit card imprint he ran through for the final bill. He also had an uncanny knack for remembering faces and names. One of the reasons he owned a bar. He knew all of his regulars, and some of his not so regulars.

"Ha. Nice try, man. I'm never at a loss for a warm body." I grabbed my bottle and turned around, surveying the filling bar. A plethora of women draped themselves across the chairs and small sofas pushed against one of the front walls, and a few others danced at high tops circling the small dance floor. The VIP section in the back held a small group of people, while the rest of the booths remained empty. I had quite the selection tonight, and Brad knew it.

I paused in mid sip of my soda as the brunette woman from the singles table passed by. She was no college girl, I'd bet my mint condition nineteen sixty-seven Ford Mustang on it. Her curves rocked the Jordache jeans hugging her ass, and in a discrete shift, I tugged at my own. Her gaze focused on the floor and not on the men checking her out as she shuffled by. Bowed shoulders and compressed lips screamed her state of mind; I wondered what asshole put that expression on her face. I drained the soda and made my way to the restrooms. I wanted to watch her from the shadows of the hallway as she returned to her friends. Women fell into my lap, literally. I needed a challenge, and I picked her.

"Would you like to dance?" My fingers tapped her shoulder as I slid into step behind her. *She's tiny. Even with high heels on.* Her "No, thank you" and shrug of my hand from her shoulder surprised me. I stepped back to one of the high tops on the edge of the dance floor and licked my wounds. I'm a patient man. Besides, I couldn't face my friends at the moment. Failure wasn't an option. Her body beneath mine filled with pleasure and an orgasmic glow lighting up her face instead of a frown remained a steadfast goal. One I intended to achieve.

Her friend winked and pointed at me during the last song. I took her cue and slid behind the brunette again, my words were spoken close to her ear in response to her comment about me. "I don't think you know my fantasy."

Her steps faltered as the guys yelled from across the bar, and she turned and tried joining her friends once more. "I'm pretty sure I know exactly your type."

Oh, really? You might be surprised. "Why don't you tell me about my type over a drink?" I grabbed her hand and pulled her from the crowded space. My body betrayed me with its agenda. This woman, in her tight jeans, high heels, and black silk shirt, called to the predator within. She snubbed me at each turn. Her future surrender intrigued me. How I achieved it, *when* I achieved it... was just a matter of time.

I stopped Brad's sister, Mandy, on my way over to the VIP section and gave her a drink order. On semester break, she agreed to help him out for a couple weeks before school started again in January. It saved Brad's ass and gave her some extra pocket money during the holidays. She nodded then walked away once I told her where I was headed.

Our sodas arrived, and my lovely companion stared at the glasses like they were poisoned apples delivered by an old crone straight from the Black Forest.

"I don't drink."

"Really?" *The empty glasses littering your table says that's a lie.*

"What is it?"

Ah. Never take a drink from a stranger. Smart girl. "Coke."

"Coke?"

"Yeah. A classic. I like classic things." *Classic cars. Classic books. Come sit on Santa's lap and tell me what you like.* "Go

ahead, try yours." I pushed it her way, and she leaned over and gave it a sniff.
Definitely has trust issues.

"Coke."

Surprise. Santa's telling the truth. "Yep. I rarely drink. I've seen too many bad things happen when people drink too much."

"Hmm."

Whoever created this level of distrust within her needed their ass kicked. I've only been nice. Yeah, I have an agenda, but I've given her no reason to judge me unfairly. "So, you new in town or just here for the holidays?" I nodded at her untouched soda.

"Your Coke. Here for—" A slideshow of emotions slid over her face before it settled on horror and set off an avalanche of fine tremors. "God, how could I be so stupid?"

I hoped her question was rhetorical because I took that moment to slurp down the rest of her Coke and grin over the straw between my lips. "Tell me what you're doing here. I can make things disappear."

Her head jerked up, and she stared at my goofy grin. Her laugh snuck out, and she covered her mouth as her ears turned a bright red.

"I like it when you laugh. It's what caught my eye when you were taking a shot back there at the table with your friends." *Well, maybe not a shot, but she definitely had a highball glass with some fruity concoction coloring it.*

"I did not take a shot."

Shit. Change of topic.

"How about you? What's your story?"

Whew. Saved by the bell.

She tilted her head toward the table where four of my crew members grinned and hooted at me from across the bar.

I squinted through the flashing lights and contemplated my payback plan as they continued cat-calling and whistling. Granted, I've been known to do the same thing to them, but this time was different. This woman was not some airhead bimbo trying to climb my body like a jungle gym and suck my tonsils out between breaths. She's educated, from what I can tell, and giving me one hell of a hard time. I peered up at the tin ceiling tiles with a sense of pride. I recreated every one by hand with a metal stamp and mallet and then painted them white, giving them a plaster appearance. I smiled and looked over the place. "I've been here on my days off helping my buddy fix and clean stuff up. They had a grease fire last month. I take it you didn't know this was the first night he's been open since the fire?"

"Interesting."

What the hell does that mean?
"Perhaps," I answered. *Christ, woman. Throw me a bone here.*

"I need to go." She scooted across the vinyl cushion and pulled the strap of her purse over her head.

Might as well go big or go home. "Tomorrow?"

"Maybe."

Holy shit, was that a yes? "Seven, I'll get us a table."

"Where?"

I have no fucking idea, but I'll think of something. "Where do I pick you up?"

"Here." She stood and, without a backward glance, waved to her friends before she strolled out the front door into the night.

I was sixteen all over again.

At six forty-five, I climbed from my car and made my way inside The Eye. Music hummed in the background, muted compared to the raucous party from the night before. Patrons filled the barstools around the glossy cherrywood stained bar and chatted with each other as Brad pulled taps and popped lids from longneck beers. He nodded at my arrival and set a glass of water out for me. "Hey, I thought you were on shift today."

I shook my head and stared at the front doors, waiting for the enigmatic woman from last night. "No, I took a couple shifts off. I'm working a job with Jordan on a spec house design." Cold water slid down my throat in an icy stream, the temperature a balm to the nerves clogging my throat. What was it about this woman that stirred the tremors in my hands and distracted me? Jordan said as much today when I botched the solar panel measurements three times on our new building design in the AutoCAD program. After the third time, he called me on my shit, and I spilled my guts like a prisoner on truth serum.

"What's going on? You're staring at the door like it's going to do a magic trick."

"You should've been a cop." I grumbled and pulled at the collar of my Izod I changed three times before yelling 'fuck-it' and tossing on a pair of beige pleated pants and my Sperry's. This was *after* I cut my face shaving and spent thirty minutes holding pressure until the bleeding stopped. Yeah, paramedic skills learned on the job came in handy at home, too.

"I'm waiting for my date. She's meeting me here at seven." I glared at the friend I've known almost as long as Jordan. Waiting for some smartass comments about my prowess and loose morals. Or, a shocking remark about more than one date with the same woman. Technically, it was two days in a row, only tonight was a date. Our only date. Just the way I liked it. One and done.

Calculation

Safe. No lingering feelings, no misinterpretations. Candace wore on me with each day she showed at the station. My conscience needed a clean sweep of her, fast.

"Ah, the goddess from last night."

His tone filled me with dread, and the glass slipped a bit in my hand. "You know her?"

His mouth tipped into a knowing grin. "I've seen her around."

"You bastard. You slept with her?" I slammed the empty glass on the bar. "Christ. Why didn't you tell me?" Customers slid covert glances my way as I yelled at Brad.

"Keep it down. I did no such thing." Brad held up a hand. "She and her friends come here once a month, sometimes more. That's all."

I dragged a hand down my face and frowned. "Sorry, man. I'm strung tighter than a kite string."

Another glass of water plopped down in front of me. "You need to get laid, Caelum. Plain and simple."

Brad's words trailed off as the door opened, and the woman from last night stepped inside. I gulped down the water and waived thanks to my friend as I made a hasty path to my date. I called for reservations at the hotel down the street. At their restaurant only, since I already had a room from the last few weeks. Hope flared inside me. I wanted to rush through dinner and spend time savoring her body for dessert. Once I slaked my needs, and she glowed with satisfaction, then we'd part ways. *One time only,* as I planned.

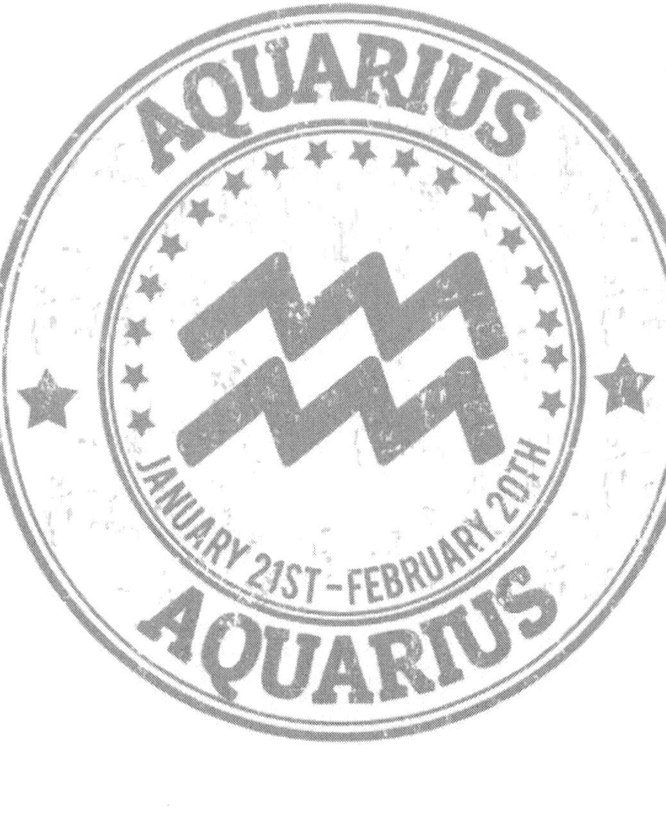
AQUARIUS
JANUARY 21ST-FEBRUARY 20TH
AQUARIUS

Chapter Four

Caelum

Her eyes flared wide when I mentioned dinner reservations at the hotel up the street. "Is that a problem?"

"No, not at all." She lifted the strap of her purse over her head and straightened her jacket as she stared toward our destination.

"Do you want me to drive, or would you prefer to meet me there?" Her brows furrowed as she plucked the button on her lapel.

"I took a taxi."

"No problem. I'm parked over there." I pulled my keys out and pointed to the navy blue and white striped fastback I spent over three years perfecting to her original beauty.

"Oh, wow. A Shelby GT500."

I skidded to a stop over some loose gravel as I stared at the enchantress running a finger along the rear quarter panel of my prized possession. Color dotted high on her cheeks as she continued her inspection from the cobra covered gas cap to the twin headlights in the center of the front grill.

"It's beautiful. Is your family the original owner?"

Her head popped up, her mouth pursed, eyes sparkling, and the uncontrolled need to kiss her senseless crept through my veins. Hell, I didn't even know her name. Yet, I've fallen a little for her because she loves my car. *Who is this woman?* "Uh, no. I bought her three years ago and restored her. She was a racecar and in pretty bad shape."

My key snicked in the lock with a twist, and I pulled the passenger door open with ease. The flowered dress she wore opened with a slit up her entire leg as it gaped wide with her smooth slide into the passenger seat. *Damn.* This woman distracted me on far too many levels. *Maybe she'd want to skip dinner and go straight to dessert?* "Buckle up," I ordered and hoped to God the erection stayed hidden behind the pleats in my pants.

The hostess led us to a table tucked into an intimate nook, away from prying eyes. I wanted her to myself without distractions grabbing her attention from me. With drinks ordered, I extended my hand and introduced myself. I'm a bastard, but, for some reason, she tempered me this evening.

"Nice to meet you, Caelum. I'm Mina." I pulled her hand close and kissed the soft skin over her knuckles. A faint lavender scent increased as the heat of my breath puffed over her.

An explosion of pink covered her cheeks as she pulled her dainty hand back and into her lap. My thoughts traveled down a dangerous road, and I wondered if the pink blush covered her entire body. Dinner evolved into a torture device tonight rather than my intended foreplay. The idea of skipping dinner and whisking her off to my room for room service played games in my mind. Visions of sucking dessert from every part of her body entertained my over-excited libido; if she'd just say *yes*. Anything to curb the ferocity of need boiling through my veins.

I adjusted myself under the tablecloth as the waiter droned on about nightly specials. Mina nodded and picked the salmon while I picked steak. I hoped they hurried. I knew watching her plump lips close over her utensils was a hazard. I'm trapped in my seat with a raging hard-on, helpless to my nature. I'm a selfish, calculating bastard. Her lip gloss needed an introduction to my shaft. Only when its slick texture covered me completely, would I be happy.

"So, you said you helped your friend fix his bar. Are you in construction?"

My attention jerked back to the beauty sitting across from me. It's not that I wasn't paying attention to her. On some level, I'm present; but for the most part, I'd planned the seduction for the rest of the night. My fingers played with the water glass on my right, sliding through the condensation ringing the glass in a soothing figure-eight pattern. "I am a licensed contractor, yes. I also work for the Portland Fire Department."

"Now, it makes sense." The tiny smile that parted her shiny lips captured my attention. I wanted those lips focused on me. *Soon.*

I leaned forward at her murmured words. "What makes sense?" A deep flush of red decorated the skin of her neck and cleavage. My mouth watered for a chance at exploring each inch of her.

"All of the eye candy last night." She giggled, and a grin tugged my mouth at the reference to the five of us as we passed by her table.

"I'll take that as a compliment."

"Hooo, yeah." Her devilish smirk remained as she fanned herself with the linen napkin. Scooping her up in a fireman carry with my hand on her ass flashed inside my head. Her final destination—my bed. I practiced that move with sandbags for months before the physical agility exam required for the firefighter position. My hand shifted to the ridge pressed against my zipper. I've practiced the hose pull all my life. A laugh spilled free at my own joke, and

I found her studying me when I met her smoke-hued gaze again.

"Hey, you have to share. What's so funny?" Her eyes scrunched up as her face brightened.

"No, you first. How do you know about the GT500?" I lobbed back with awe tinting my voice.

"Here you are. Salmon for the lady. The filet for the gentleman."

Damn it.

Our waiter picked that exact moment to deliver our dinner. Finally, when I'd learn a tiny piece of information about the alluring woman seated across from me. Electricity pulsed through my veins in equal parts of frustration and excitement. The sooner we finished, the faster my name became a repeat of pants slipping from her lips.

"Oh, that's good."

A sip became my entire drink as she moaned around her fork. Innocent expression of pleasure? I'm not sure since I'm treading in uncharted waters. Something I'm unfamiliar with. Her short answers lack the engagement of friends sharing conversation over a nice meal. Even though I plan never to see her again, I enjoy conversation and learning about others. This reminds me of spy movies where each character plots their next move around body language and carefully revealed clues. I catch the smirk hidden behind her napkin as she dabs her lips in a poor excuse of subterfuge. My body jolts to attention, and I'm jacked higher than a cocaine addict. Conversation between us ended. An overrated expectation in my book. Words fell flat when her body spoke the truth she wouldn't reveal.

"Would you care for coffee or dessert?"

I praised the higher power as she shook her head. I can't leave here soon enough. I licked my plate clean in less than fifteen minutes. Rude? Maybe. But, my plans were worth their weight in gold. "No, thank you. Please charge this to my room." I caught the tilt of her head and press of her lips. "It's not like that, really. I work every third day at the fire station. This saved me an hour commute daily while I was working on the repairs at the bar."

"Oh."

I'm losing her. Delicate lines of dismay creased her forehead like a book. Granted, I could've checked out of my room days ago, yet, I kept it for one more weekend. I understood the opinion she jumped to about me at the moment. "Come on. Let's go for a walk." I stood and offered my hand.

The hotel set a light display up for Christmas that snaked through the property. Holding her hand sounded nice, and hopefully, she'd offer me more than that. I helped her with her coat and shrugged into mine as we stepped out into

Calculation

the brisk air. With my hand settled on her lower back, I noticed the shivers racking her body. What started out as a leisurely stroll now ended in less than five minutes. *Damn it.*

"As much as I'd like to see the lights, you aren't dressed for winter sightseeing tonight." I gathered her frozen hand into mine and reentered the heated lobby.

"What *am* I dressed for?"

Her whispered words jump-started my heart. I pulled her close and escorted her toward the bank of elevators. My answer to her question also a whisper. "My hope is that you aren't dressed for long."

I sucked on the lobe of her ear, around the little diamond stud she wore, then kissed down her neck as the elevator took its sweet time to our location. The sigh she breathed out when the silver doors finally opened surprised me. With a strength I wasn't expecting, she pushed me against the elevator wall and slid her hands under my shirt. I barely got the button for my floor pressed before she lifted my shirt and started sucking at the exposed skin.

"Shit, Mina. You gotta hold on, baby. Not here." I grinned up at the camera dome in the elevator ceiling as her fingers skated along the waistband of my pants, yanking at the button and metal clasp holding them closed. A bell dinged overhead, and the doors slid open.

Thank Fuck.

I scooped her little body up in my arms and raced down the corridor to my room. She bit and sucked at the skin of my neck, and I almost dropped her when the key fell out of my hand. "Baby, I have to put you down."

Her mewl stirred crazy, primal desires within me. I paused for a deep breath before I broke the key, shaking in my hand, off in the lock. The door flew open, and her dress was up and over her head before it slammed closed. Elegant satin and lace greeted my mouth as I dove for the nipples jutting through the transparent material.

Her fingers worked on the buttons lining my shirt without success. I needed to feel her skin on mine. The frenzy of her movements ramped the desire firing like molten lava through my veins. I pulled away from the feast at my fingertips and jerked the shirt over my head, saving her the effort.

"Oh my."

I preened under her gaze, but she wasn't admiring my gym work. The steel spike present during dinner grabbed her attention. If her lip gloss came anywhere close to me right now, I'd lose my man card. As much as I wanted to take her mouth, I was out of patience. Air whooshed between my teeth as she slid my zipper and wrapped her tiny hand around me. I twitched and covered her hand with mine. "You first."

Her chin tilted, and her pupils dilated in the dim lighting.

I knelt on the floor and removed her shoes, then hooked my fingers in the transparent lace hiding the reward I desired. It slid across her satiny skin and fluttered to the floor like a butterfly. I lifted each foot free from the silky trappings, then kissed her belly and licked a path between her breasts. Each strap of her barely-there bra fell as I tugged them off her shoulders with my teeth. She twirled in my arms, and I cupped her breasts before I worked the hooks free. Completely bared to me, I spun her once again. *Finally.*

Her head fell back as I sucked one, then the other, nipple deep into my mouth. Little moans floated from her lips on the heated air. My body strained for hers as I slid my hands over the landscape of perfect skin, sweat beading on my brow as I held back. Tremors wracked her legs, and I scooped her up and placed her onto the bed.

I needed her healthy and whole, not rug burned from the pace I'd set. She licked her lips, and lust flared from her gaze as I revealed the aching part of me that needed her most. I crawled up her needy body, leaving a trail of kisses everywhere but where she wanted. Once I met her lips, I dove in and started my exploration. The friction of her skin on mine—*heaven*.

My lips and tongue traveled on a journey of her hills and valleys, having left no stone unturned. Fingers explored hidden caves as my tongue strummed her body like a raging waterfall. Before she exploded, I rolled protection on and slid into her molten heat. I loomed over her as I slowly built her back up, grinding into her sweet spot with deep thrusts. I slipped her leg over my hip and stared into her passion-filled eyes. Eyes that sucked you in like quicksand; deep into the center of the earth. Deep into the center of her soul. Vanilla burst over my tongue as I nipped at her bee-stung lips. The gloss I admired earlier, a smooth glide between us. As I parted her lips and dove inside for her secrets, my wits returned with the loss of my rhythm.

No! What did I just do?

She gasped and gripped me tightly. I tumbled over with her as she moaned and shook in my arms. Her swollen lips stared back at me when I recovered and finally opened my eyes. While I'd regret my lapse of rigid personal standards any other time, now, I puffed my tail like a peacock. Whisker burns marked her neck in trails of red streaks of ownership. Mine burned with the memory of her stinging bites. Twin stamps of possession decorated our skin. Something I'd never experienced nor

Calculation

desired before. This woman, Mina, crashed through the walls I carefully built over many years like they were tissue paper. Nothing.

"Hey, where did you go?"

Eyes at half-mast, she stared at me as I slid from the heat of her body. I craved her like a drug and needed another connection now that I slipped free. I dipped low for another chance at possessing her mouth. As we surfaced for a breath, I whispered, "Absolutely nowhere."

With a flick of my wrist, I tossed the condom and rolled close, tucking her head into the crook of my neck. Our skin formed a sticky bond where we touched, yet I didn't care. I pulled the blanket up and over the both of us as we drifted off, relaxed and replete.

───

I stretched and eased the fog from my sleep-deprived brain. A satisfied smile stretched my lips as I rolled to the soft, warm body next to me. Memories of last night fueled new ones, and I pulled the pillow from between us with every intention of continuing where we left off. "What the hell?" With a snap of my wrist, the bedside lamp flared bright over the room. A distinct chill filled the empty space, and silence greeted my blurry vision. Instead of the sexy goddess from last night, a folded piece of paper occupied the space where Mina's head rested between short naps and marathon sex. I grabbed the piece of hotel stationery and prayed for a 'Hail Mary' instead of a 'Dear John' letter.

Caelum,

Thank you for a lovely evening. I'm visiting family for the holidays and won't return until after Christmas. If you aren't busy for New Year's Eve, I'd like to invite you out for dinner this time. Meet me in the hotel bar at seven p.m. on New Year's Eve. Leave a note at the front desk if you are otherwise previously engaged.

Mina

I fisted the morning wood tenting the comforter over my lap. "Lovely evening?" I groaned as my hand slid over the silky smooth residual of lip gloss. "It was fucking spectacular." If I couldn't have the real thing this morning, I'd make do with the vanilla gloss and the image of her lips

Calculation

stretched around me. If she thought I wouldn't show, she was sorely mistaken. No one *ever* left me, I left them. Payback in kind trickled through my brain. Sex her up, then leave *without* a note. I needed a raincheck on my vow of one and done. This was an exception. *After* my night paying her back, I'd leave and never come back.

I jumped out of bed and headed for the shower. I needed hot water and *a lot* of soap.

"Hey, Jordan. What's up?" The refrigerator closed with a nudge of my hip as I answered the phone and popped the tab from a Coke.

"Hey, Cal. Bart wanted me to call and see what your plans are for New Year's."

Jordan's chuckle raised the hairs on my arms. The last time he laughed like that, the psycho bridesmaid from his wedding arrived at my fire station and didn't leave until I practically threw her out. "Uh, is this a trick question? I don't like the tone of your voice."

Less mad scientist than his previous laugh, Jordan's chuckle still rang with a tinge of malevolence and self-assuredness. "She thinks she's actually going to stay awake long enough to ring in the new year. After throwing up for several hours in the morning, a couple cat naps, and me rubbing her back after dinner, she hasn't made it past nine, in weeks."

It was my turn to laugh. Married for almost five months, his wife was four months pregnant and dealing with a varying severity of morning sickness. Jordan was beside himself and turned into an alpha asshole. Working with him on the spec house job tested my patience when he got into one of his moods.

"Well, turns out I'm going to dinner again with the chick I met last week." I pulled the phone from my ear then pressed it against the other side. "Hello? Jordan? Are you still there?" Silence greeted me from his end. I turned to hang up and call him back when his voice cracked over the open line.

"As I live and breathe, I never thought I'd see it. Pigs do fly."

Jordan snickered as I coughed and choked on a huge mouthful of Coke. His comment a shot right to the solar plexus and thought-provoking for a very, *very* long minute of my current single life. "Hardy, har, har. You're such a comedian."

"What, babe?" Bart's voice in the background filtered over the phone line in a series of 'wha wha wha' sounds, just like the adults sounded in the old Peanuts cartoons. "Oh, that's a good one. Excellent memory, babe. Bart wants to know if you kissed her yet?"

Holy shit!

"Uh, kiss—" Another coughing fit wracked my chest, this time due to the sudden sand storm sucking all the moisture from my body. "Kissed her? Why would I kiss her?"

"You were right, babe," Bart commented again; I strained to decipher her comment. "Yeah, I agree with you. Now, go get on the couch. I'll be there in a few."

"Agree with her? About what? It's not like that." I assured him, yet, a cold shiver climbed my spine as I pictured Mina spread before me, her eyes blazing with her fierce need. Me growling back at her, my jaw clenched as I brought her to heaven and back over and over, before I jumped, too.

Through gritted teeth, my lie spilled out, "She's a fuck buddy. We met, we ate, we fucked. Now, we're on a rinse and repeat cycle."

"Uh, huh. The gent doth protest too much, methinks."

"Don't quote Shakespeare to me, asshole. I was in the same class as you." I set my can on the kitchen counter, my knuckles white as I gripped the edge of the sink and stared out the window. *What am I doing? I've got to tread carefully here. I don't want a repeat of psycho Candy.*

Jordan's cough sounded suspiciously like a suppressed laughter. "So, I'll tell Bart you can't make it, then?" With a sigh, my head drooped forward in resignation. The happily married couple won this round. Any more protests on my behalf gave them more cannon fodder.

"Tell her I'm sorry. I'll make it up to her another day." I took another swig of my tepid cola and resumed my kitchen window vigil. I couldn't put a finger on why their comment crawled under my skin and festered like a splinter. The two of them made my teeth hurt with how syrupy sweet they were to each other. Not everyone found their happily ever after.

"Caelum. You kissed her, didn't you?"

Jordan and I both groaned and whined Bart's name as another house extension clicked over with her rapid-fire questions, causing me to flinch and tip my can into the sink. "What? I want to hear it from him. Mr. I-never-fuck-the-same-woman-twice is having dinner with the same woman. Spill it, buddy."

"I think it's the only way she'll shut up, Cal. Just answer the hormone-crazed woman, then I'll take over and occupy her thoughts instead of you." Jordan and Bart grumbled back and forth as I twisted the time I spent with Mina through my brain.

"It's awfully quiet on your side, Caelum?"

Calculation

"Okay, fine. You're right, Bart. I kissed her. You happy? It was a spur of the moment thing; I didn't think anything about it. But I did it. So, there." I flung the empty can across the kitchen where it banked off the wall and into the trash. Such a smug couple. So sure that a meaningless action on my part coalesced into something deep and philosophical between Mina and me.

"You like her-rrr," Bartlett sang out like a kid on the playground.

"Bart, I went out with her one time. She's nice. The sex was great. What else does there need to be?"

"You kissed her and had sex? Damn, brother."

"Ah, Jesus. *Fuck*. The two of you. Just stop, alright? I'm a grown-ass man. I don't need the two of you meddling. I'm just fine where I'm at." My fingers ripped through the hair at my temple, the little bite of pain centering me.

"Caelum, I love you like my big brother. I want you to be happy. That's all I wish for you. Well, and I want to meet her."

"Bart, go get on the couch, now! Let me talk to my friend for a minute." Jordan ordered Bart, and the extension clicked— but not before an irritated huff.

"You know she means well? Sometimes she's not subtle. I find more so now that she's pregnant. Like her belly is a superpower, and everyone must bow to her will." I shook my head at the thought of Jordan bending to anyone's will.

"Well, I can't imagine having this same conversation with my mother. So, I'm thankful in that regard." The phone cord hooked on the refrigerator handle, and I twirled it like a jump rope to free it.

"Hey, Cal?"

"Yeah?"

"Be careful and take it one day at a time. Something's different this time. Bart's not the only one who noticed."

"Thanks, man. I'll take your advice under consideration." The line clicked to a dial tone as I rolled his words around in my head. Denial of everything they hinted at surged through me. This was payback for leaving me high and dry. That's all it was.

∿∿
∿∿

The elevator bell dinged as it stopped at the lobby level. Memories from the last time I stepped inside the metal box swirled inside my brain. How the night ended in the drunken throes of our bodies, minds, and mouths searching for more within one another, yet her morning disappearing act still rattled my cage. A familiar tap of shoes on the terracotta tile jarred me back to reality, and I stepped out into the crowded space. Guests milled back and forth, dressed in their most elegant party attire of tuxedos and sequin-embellished dresses. The hotel's bar, Pelo del Perro, and our designated meeting space, faced the lobby. Mina declared our location and time, so I waded through the busy space for the entrance. I wanted the pleasure of stripping her with my eyes before she saw me.

A soda in my hand, my back pressed against one of the faux painted pillars waiting for her arrival. The tie wrapped around the collar of my suit cinched like a noose around my neck, and I prayed for relief from its binding hold sooner than later. I pulled at the knot in vain as the tension of her arrival built within me. The cobalt blue color was a particular purchase, only meant as a placeholder for my suit. Its intention far more practical in my eyes when it decorated my date later.

Its color reminded me of the flowers on Mina's dress and how she'd slid into my car and shown me just a slice of the hidden treasure beneath them. Ice cubes clinked against my glass as I drained the fizzy liquid and placed it on the table next to me. My fingers drummed with an impatient tap against the watch at my wrist as I shifted back and forth on the balls of my feet. Only a few minutes separated me from my New Year's goal; the last week an exercise in patience and self-flagellation. A flurry of activity caught my eye as a woman in a painted-on dress entered amid murmured catcalls of "Hola, Mami" and discrete wolf whistles. Two men approached and stopped in her path, blocking most of her from my view.

My curiosity piqued as sequins flashed, and bare skin peeked through the black material lit from the overhead can lights. As she brushed by the men, her dress winked into full view. Practically sheer, only opaque geometric shapes covered the money shots, while sequins distracted the eye from the naked skin below. I stood up straighter and blinked twice when the beauty gave a secret smile and walked my way. *Mina? Fuck, me.*

Painted red toenails in skyscraper heels complemented the curve-hugging, sequined dress and matching clutch as she stopped in front of me. Before my little brain took complete control, I cupped her jaw and once again did something spontaneous and against my own rules: placed a kiss on the edge of her mouth. "Let's save all of that lipstick for later. I don't want to waste a bit of it." Her lips curved into a knowing smile that had me itching for more of her now, rather than later. Food was overrated.

"I'm hungry now. Let's order room service."

Fuck, yes.

Calculation

She sucked in a breath as I pulled her close and slid a thumb over a gauzy nipple. "Do I get dessert first?"

In a sultry voice, she whispered, "I'm an all you can eat buffet. It doesn't matter if you start with dessert or the main course. You only have to peel back the wrapper to get to the sweet center."

Her mouth called to me, and I pulled her in for another chaste kiss as her fingers slid inside my jacket and yanked at the belt around my waist. With a toothy grin to the bystanders gawking at us, I wrapped an arm around her shoulders and directed her toward the exit, where I hoped some of my sanity remained. As we crossed through the doorway, I nipped her ear and whispered, "Let's get you upstairs and those legs wrapped around my face. I want dessert first."

"So impatient."

"I missed breakfast last week. Call me selfish."

A thumb, roughened by years of work, slid back and forth over the soft skin of her bare shoulder as we shared the elevator with an older couple. The woman frowned and checked out Mina as we stepped inside, her opinion of Mina's dress mixed from the sidelong glances she kept shooting our way.

My words came out in a husky whisper as I leaned close and inhaled the sweet gardenia scent of her hair. Her proximity left me lightheaded and unsteady on my feet like a drug. "I'm glad you're in front of me. I'm afraid I'd ruin your fancy dress if we were alone." Goosebumps traveled down her arm as I traced the line of fabric scooping low along her bare back. "It looks like someone made it just for you. Gorgeous. A bit risqué for this crowd, but tasteful in the placement of the designs." My whispered words breathed along the edge of her jaw as I drew a line straight down her spine. "Wanna know what my favorite part of it is?" Mina tilted on her feet as I pulled her into my chest and growled, "It fits you like a fucking glove. Just like you fit me."

With a discrete shift of her heel, she ground against the ridge of steel settled against the small of her back.

"You're breathtaking."

Once the couple exited, I pinned Mina's hands behind my neck and slid the greedy free fingers of the other inside the back of her dress. They traveled over her silky smooth skin and found the nipples straining for attention. "Hmm. I'll have to suck on those too."

"Oh, God."

Her head fell onto my chest as I rolled and pinched each side into tight little buds. Gasps and soft moans followed my nimble fingers as her ass ground into my erection without remorse. "Now who's impatient?

Next floor is mine." I whispered into the shell of her ear as I slid a hand lower and discovered nothing impeding my way.

My floor arrived as she moaned and strained against me. With a flourish, I gripped her hand and nabbed her purse from the floor where it landed as I held her hostage in my arms. "I'm at the end of the hall. Room 730."

"Hang on." She pulled us to a stop, slipped off her shoes, and handed them to me. "I'll race you."

With a girly shriek, she took off. A cocky grin crept into place as I watched her lift her dress away from her legs. She couldn't beat me. I swam and ran cross country all through high school and college. My crew and I ran half marathons once or twice a year for the firefighter charities. Her head start wouldn't hurt me a bit. She squeaked as I thundered up behind her and scooped her up and over my shoulder right before she touched the door. I palmed her ass and handed her purse and shoes to her as I dug out my key and let us into the suite I reserved.

"Wow, this is nice." She dropped from my shoulder and padded around the small table set for two. A dining cart sat to the side with covered dishes and a bottle of wine, while a bucket with champagne on ice chilled on a separate cart with strawberries and several desserts covered in clear domes.

Two floating candles bobbed in glass holders and cast flickering bits of light off the view of Portland in the floor-to-ceiling windows she gazed through. "Come join me?" She offered her hand as I filled water glasses at our table.

Her question struck me as odd. Gone was her playful, assertive self, and in her place was someone off balance. Insecure, *no*, unsure, if I read my instincts right. I crossed my arms and gave her a mocked scowl. "I'm sure there's a please in there somewhere."

Her body weaved in the backlit skyline as a shudder flowed through her. "Please, Caelum?"

Thank God. I'm about to punch a hole through my suit pants. "My pleasure."

Before I realized, I ditched my jacket and loosened my tie, then knelt in front of her. Skimming up her perfect legs, I slowly drew her dress up and then over the jeweled clips holding her thick hair. Completely bare to me, her cinnamon-tinted areolas puckered as I pressed her against glass chilled by the December air. Goosebumps pebbled her skin as I skimmed my lips down the slope of her neck, leaving marks of possession with slight stinging bites. Her taut nipples begged for attention as I pulled one, then the other between my lips with relish. My tongue swirled around each blood-filled peak until her legs scissored

Calculation

together, searching for the right friction. "You are so beautiful." Tremors ran through her legs as I lifted one, then the other, over my shoulders, and pressed her fully against the glass as I completely devoured her.

Her fingers scrambled for purchase in my hair as her body hurdled forward, out of control, yet I steered the helm.

"Oh, God."

I paused, arrogance dripping from my words. "I am tonight."

Her back bowed, and she shattered as two fingers nudged inside her and stroked the bundle of nerves made just for her pleasure. I took everything she gave me as she writhed and convulsed with the strength of her climax. I eased my pressure and supported her back as I lifted her into my arms and away from the freezing window. She hung limp in my arms, content for the moment. Now relaxed, I planned to tie her to my bed and savor dinner, served from her body.

"Hey, what are you doing?"

A disadvantage of hotel rooms, they didn't have true headboards. I had arrived much earlier in the day and rigged a pulley for my wily date. Moving her to the bed, I positioned her on her back, legs spread, and created a slipknot with my tie. I had her under lock and key, so to speak. "I didn't want you escaping when I wasn't looking."

Lids clattered as I shuffled through the selection of items I chose for ease of clean up and versatility in temperature. Some of it might end up cold before we got to it. A smirk shifted into place as I covered everything back up and grabbed a napkin.

Eyes wide and pupils blown, I caught a look of terror on her face as she flinched when I turned with her plate.

"What's wrong?" My smug look of triumph evaporated in the tension-filled space between us.

Tears welled in her eyes, and *I knew*. My selfish desire to keep her close just fucked me six days from Sunday. "Shit, Mina. I'm so sorry." I dropped her plate on the table and fumbled with the knots at her wrists. "I'd never hurt you."

I backed away in horror as she pulled the sheet over her body. *What the fuck did I just do?* Her dress laid in a heap next to one of her shoes, and I searched the floor for its match. Anything to avoid the accusation and fear staring back at me from the woman that so recently gazed at me with stars in her eyes, drunk with pleasure. *Very serial killer, Caelum. You are one Class-A bastard.*

Shoes in hand, I placed them, and her dress, next to her, then backed away. "I've never acted like this before. Scaring you was the furthest thing from my mind tonight." Lights winked in the distance as I moved to

Calculation

where just minutes ago—minutes that felt like days—I'd held her in my arms and felt like a king. A king with his queen, high in a castle where they wanted for nothing other than each other. Now all I saw was smudged glass and a man filled with regrets mirrored there. A mechanical hum of the heater cut into the silence of my thoughts. "There's something about you that makes me irrational. I'm one of the safest, sanest, and calmest people on the planet. I have to be. People—*my crew*—can die if I'm not. God, Mina. I'm so, so sorry." The same fingers that provided pleasure and pain raked through my hair. My reflection now a vision of suffering and remorse.

"What do you want from me?"

Her timid voice halted the furious thoughts swarming like angry bees in a perpetual loop. A frustrated breath fogged the window. *What the fuck **do** you want, Caelum?* "Honestly?" I approached her like a wounded animal and sat at the edge of the bed. Her hands felt like ice as I pulled them into mine. My thumbs found the red chafed skin and gingerly traced it around her wrists. "I'd like to have dinner with you and talk a little bit. Maybe you'll even stay the night?" I moved a little closer and placed her hands on my chest. "Be here in the morning and have breakfast with me? You left last time—" I put it all out there. My ego had nothing to lose now. "I don't want that again."

Typically, my Aquarius nature had every scenario planned out; what I didn't plan on was frightening her. I had no intent to harm her so that never crossed my mind. Now an evening of food and great company collapsed into a flaming inferno. I lifted her wrists and kissed each one. "I swear to you; I'm telling the truth. I'd never hurt you. I took an oath to protect lives and property. I take that part of me very seriously."

Her fingers tightened over mine, and hope flared brightly. Brown eyes peeked out under mascara-tipped lashes as she tipped her face. "I'd hate for you to waste all that food and the great view."

Her lopsided grin punched me like a sledgehammer, and I heaved a sigh. "From where I was at, the view was amazing."

"I bet."

Her pulse trilled under my fingers. At least somewhat forgiven for my massive blunder if the heightened color of her cheeks was any indication. "Really. It was. I dare say it was even interactive."

With a groan, she pulled free and covered her face. "Was I really that loud? I'm so embarrassed."

"On the contrary, not loud enough." I plucked her fingers free and kissed the tip of her nose. "Since you didn't scream, I didn't do a good enough job." I tried not to laugh at the shocked look on her face. "I must try again and reclaim my honor."

I knelt on the floor next to the bed and bowed over her hand. "My Lady, please allow me to keep trying until I perform to your utmost satisfaction."

Her snort of laughter thawed a part of me I kept isolated from the world. The idealistic part of me. The part that believed in goodwill, love, and commitment, without all of the ugly parts of humanity.

"I suppose I can suffer through your ministrations as you endeavor for the favor of my hand." I kept a straight face as she burst out laughing once again, mocking my attempt at a knight in shining armor as she slid into a southern belle. Joy looked good on her. I'm glad this moment of levity brought something fun to the disastrous situation I caused.

"What are your qualifications?" She pretended to take notes on an invisible piece of paper. "I must know if you have an aptitude for the job."

Her words, spoken with a sultry Georgian accent, were sexy as fuck. I really wanted to rock her world. I appreciated achievable goals, especially when I gained from the outcome, too. I sucked at accents, so I leaned toward my assets. "Well, ma'am..." I unbuttoned my shirt and shrugged it off. "...I keep my body in tip-top condition." My bicep bulged as I flexed the muscle. "Feel it."

She sat up, and the sheet slipped from her grasp. With a wink, she stood and put her breasts in my face as she pushed on my arm. With a sniff, she sat back down and asked, "Is that all? Surely you have more endearing qualities than that."

I moved to the side of the bed and removed my shoes and socks. With a wink of my own, I wiggled my toes. "I have big...hands."

"Do you now? How will that help me decide?" She pulled my hand into her lap and compared hers to mine.

"I'd have to demonstrate for the full effect." My fingers curled into a 'C' shape, and I swear she whispered 'My God' in Spanish.

"Everything you offer is all fine attributes, sir. Yet, none singularly seem up to the task." She tipped her head to the side as she dragged a finger up my bare chest. "Am I to wonder what other untold pleasures you hide from me?" Her eyes spent a lazy minute drinking me in.

"If your chaperone will allow it, would you accompany me to dinner? I assure you the conversation will be stimulating, and, I daresay, even scandalous." I nodded at the fluttering candles and plates sitting empty in front of the chairs.

Calculation

"Oh, dear. You must feed me, or I shall faint in anticipation."

I offered my hand and pulled her upright with a smile. Rather than pulling a sheet from the bed, I picked my shirt up and offered it to her like a coat. She shrugged into it as I once again knelt in front of her and fastened buttons too large for her tiny body. I folded the cuffs and stood to admire my work. "Hmm. Almost."

She stared down at the shirt then at me. "What's wrong?"

I flicked the top five buttons open so it gaped good and wide. "I'll miss the view."

"Oh, my."

"I did say scandalous." I wagged my eyebrows at her bared breasts.

"You, sir, are a rake."

Our banter lasted through the main entree until a giggle interrupted a long pause. The pause on my part, since, apparently, she excelled in southern colloquialisms and I didn't. A strawberry landed in my lap as I wracked my brain for something witty. With one eyebrow raised in challenge, she squealed as I jumped from my seat and chased her around the dinner table. Another first for me, chasing a half-naked, strawberry throwing, second date around a hotel suite as she giggled. With a feint to my left, she ran right into my open arms as I jumped right.

"I declare, what strong arms you have." Her snort sent her into another fit of giggles, and I swept her into my arms and over to the couch.

"I'll be right back. Don't move." I pointed to the cushion then tried and failed to hide a grin through the scowl I painted on my face.

"What happens if I move?"

I raised an eyebrow at her breathy response then raked my gaze up her barely clothed body. "It's top secret. Need to know basis only."

"Oh, you!"

I returned with a spare comforter and settled against the armrest. Hope stirred in my chest since dinner didn't end with me calling the scene defensive or my plans a total loss of person and property. The person I desired leaned against me on the sofa as we waited to welcome in the New Year with a great view of fireworks exploding across the Portland sky. No champagne in lieu of a clear head on my part. One bad decision was enough. Neither of us needed a repeat of earlier. Her little body tucked between my legs with my arms holding her close satisfied me in more ways than I wanted to admit.

"Did you always want to be a firefighter?"

"Hmm." I pulled the comforter higher as she shivered in my thin shirt. "Yeah, I did. I think all little kids imagine it. What solidified it for me was a TV show I watched when I was little. I so wanted to be Johnny Gage. Drive up in a fire truck and save the day, then date the hot nurse, Dixie."

"Emergency?" She turned in my arms. "I watched it too."

"Rampart, this is Squad fifty-one." I mimicked a handheld radio as I stared into her eyes and repeated the famous line.

"Good Lord above." She fanned her face, and my question from earlier answered itself in the wave of pink blooming across her chest. "That was hot."

"I have my moments." With a peck to her nose, I twirled her back around and tucked her under the covers. "What about you? What did you want to be when you grew up?" Silence filled the space between us as I waited. Her fingers worked furiously under the blanket, yet I continued to twirl a lock of her hair without changing my pace or position. She gave nothing away except the small tell of her hands. I knew nothing about her, an odd thing since women were notorious talkers. A few things I could guess, but the rest? No clue. What she hid in that big brain of hers scared her. Not me.

I did enough damage earlier. I hoped she shared something with me.

"I wanted to be Jaime Sommers."

"Bionic woman, huh? Nice."

"Yeah, that, and I loved tennis." Her fingers stilled as we lapsed into another pause, the fireworks popping off in the distance as the clock crept closer to midnight. "I really sucked at tennis."

A laugh rumbled in my chest at her honest answer. Picturing her with a racket in her hand chasing after a yellow ball didn't fit how I imagined her. She'd be a great lawyer or public speaker. Her confidence and presence demanded your attention. She carried herself as if nothing mattered except where she ended up. And when she arrived, her focus centered only on you or the task at hand. She was strong, yet, this moment showed a softer side of her, and I was honored to be with her. "Yeah, I can't see you playing tennis. I'd step all over you. You're so tiny."

"That's only because you're a freaky giant."

Her snappy reply had me laughing once again. I'd give it to her; she was quick on her feet. *Me too*. I had her up and flipped around on my lap, facing me before she took her next snarky breath. The 'O' of her lips a pleasant reminder of a night together that seemed so long ago. "I thought we fit together pretty well."

Calculation

Her hair fell in luxurious waves of silk as I slipped the clips holding it back from me onto the floor. My borrowed shirt gaped open; the sight of her bare skin welcomed, and its access unfettered. In this moment, she looked upon me with desire, not fear as before. Like a train wreck you couldn't stop watching, she leaned forward, and I was swept away.

Soft and sweet like the strawberry she aimed at me, her lips demanded an answer. Something I was afraid and excited to provide. With a growl, I cupped her neck and deepened the kiss, my lips and tongue invading her space and expecting the same in return. This wasn't a kiss of a couple in love, this was brutal and unyielding. Punishing and messy. We breathed each other in as we gnashed our teeth and demanded more. Buttons flew as I ripped the shirt off and tossed it away. I needed her close. Her skin on mine. Like a drug, she sucked me in and made everything better. Brighter. Softer.

My heart slammed against my ribs as I let her nimble fingers work the clasp at my waist. Without words, she had me stripped and kissing her once again as I lost myself to her wonder and slid home. Home. Something my heart wanted, and she gave. The only woman I ever kissed like that, and the only woman who I both loved and hated at the same time for making me fall in love.

As grey light filtered into our room, I stretched, excited for the new day. Excited about what I learned as I worshiped Mina into the early hours of New Year's Day. My stomach growled its demands as I pushed the pillow from between us. Breakfast in bed before breakfast sounded amazing. Something I only wanted to share with her and no one else, from this day forward. She may not know it yet, but I did.

"Baby, are you awake?" A nest of pillows met my fingers, and I sat up. Deja vu played a nasty game with me as I found her side of the bed empty. I turned to look toward her pillow and searched the floor next to the bed in despair. This time, she didn't leave me a note.

AQUARIUS

JANUARY 21ST – FEBRUARY 20TH

AQUARIUS

Chapter Five

Ximena

"Are you in here again?" Julie passed through the staff bathroom as water splashed up on my face.

"Yeah. I just can't seem to shake this flu."

"Come on, it's nearly Saint Patrick's Day. You've been sick since January."

My eyes rolled, and another wave of nausea rumbled through my stomach and up my throat. There was nothing left as I dry heaved over the sink. Tears burned as they poured out past my lashes and straight into the basin.

Julie's hand rubbed a circle on my lower back. "I think you need to make a doctor's appointment."

"At the OB?" Shelley barked across the small staff bathroom with Melody on her heels.

"I know you have an OB at home in Napa, but for God's sake, Ximena. You've lived here since college. I have a great woman I can call and get things set up." I nodded in agreement.

"Good. You've looked like shit for weeks now. The parents are getting concerned, too."

A choked, "Thanks," snapped out as they continued watching me heave.

"Great idea, babe. Dr. Ashton is amazing." Julie reached for another paper towel and placed the dampened cloth on the back of my neck.

Melody and I roomed together in college. She came out of the closet during our junior year after a drunk night when she told me Charles was using me. I think I said, "How would you know since you've never dated?" and that's when she told me about her and Julie. Julie already worked at Shepherds of the Cloth; she's two years older and was Melody's big sister in their sorority.

"Fine. Make the call, but I'm not going to hear those words you all think I'm going to hear."

The heart monitor soothed me through each swish of the fast-paced *lub-dub* resonating through the exam room. The memory of how I ended up here in a fetal stress test freshly passed through my mind as the warm gel squirted onto my taught round belly.

"Your blood pressure looks good. So does the little one's." Dr. Ashton rubbed a wand along my belly. Eight days overdue, and this little boxer of my rib cage held tight to the current spa of a house it's currently cocooned in, with no thought of evacuating.

Calculation

"Let me just check the progress of your cervix, and then we can set an induction date for Wednesday or Thursday. Still sure you don't want to know the sex?"

Her loose use of the word sex throws me back momentarily to the carnal passion behind my New Year's Eve tryst, which landed me with the super sperm finding its way to the meet and greet in my ovaries. I shook my head, thinking about how brazen I was after my phone call to Charles. Who knew the mission I had devised would backfire royally, and it would be the last time I had sex.

"Positive." Then the timeline hits like a ton of bricks. "That's like three days. I can't go any further. Please, get this alien out of me."

She chuckled. "If you think you're the first mom to tell me that... Speaking of which, when I met you, your dog was going through cancer treatments. How's she doing."

I knew all too well how this small talk went when my knees shifted up on the table, and she reached under the blanket across my lap to check my cervix. It's always awkward to talk while fingers are—I must be losing my shit as the only thing crossing my mind belonged to the deft fingers of the man who shared half the genetics with this beast inside me.

"Good news. Your dilation is a solid three, effaced to about sixty percent. And you're soft. Let me strip these final membranes..." My brain stopped listening with each swipe of the more vigorous exam. "So, Sadie, how's she doing. Did you set her up for the arrival like I told you to?" The snap of her glove and water running refocused me back to the current situation.

"Sadie—yeah, she's got a clean bill of health since the removal of one of her toes and a few chemo appointments. I thought I lost her last year. And I followed the advice of making her a part of this whole experience, including smelling all the bedding, clothes, and toys."

"Make sure you send home some of the hospital blankets with the baby's scent before you actually get released from the hospital." She offered her clean hand and helped me up, since I'm turtled and can't lift myself off her table easily.

With my file in her hand and her pen jotting a few notes, she returned to the serious side of things. "With your current stats, I'm putting in orders for you to be checked in at the hospital Thursday. If I were to place a bet, I think I'll see you later tonight or tomorrow. I'm on call, so don't worry."

My hand rubbed down the side of my rib cage as the alien stretched itself across my pelvis, bladder, and ribcage. "I can do this if

Calculation

I have a set goal," I repeated this to myself with false bravado.

"Who's joining you in the delivery room?" She pushed her glasses up her nose and waited.

I sighed. "I wanted my mom, but she can't get here because of my dad's accident. So my friends Julie, Melody, and Shelley. I guess."

"Let's be clear. You need someone there to help. It keeps things smooth for you. I know we haven't discussed this, but did you reach out to the father?"

My hips wiggled themselves off the table with thoughts of the father and the few nights I carelessly followed my heart into something intended as a rebound. My hands rested on the results. "No." He wouldn't know my name anyway. I called myself Mina to protect my careless and casual fling from becoming a reality. A reality who now occupied my waistline.

"Think about the birth certificate and Social Security number information as well. I'd also suggest someone stick close. You have that labor look about you."

Birth certificate. You'd need to know their last name and how to spell their first to add the proper father to the document. *Caelum.* If that was even his real name. Who was I kidding? I deliberately set myself up for no strings attached. Never in my life had

I been as brazen as I was those few glorious days— me in control and a man who handled the bait perfectly.

"I will. I hope to see you sooner rather than Thursday." Each waddled step away from her office, I breathed harder, and the panic of motherhood set in.

Funny how things changed in a blink of an eye last year: Sadie in surgery the last day of school, Charles leaving town as soon as he knew she was ill. Then a phone call from one hotel room to the other. It shouldn't piss me off his secretary answered the phone at two in the morning New York time. It only confirmed what I already knew. Somewhere in the recesses of my mind, I understood Charles held onto me because of my family and not me. Money made for a strange bedfellow, and I think Charles prayed I'd find my way out of my teaching position and back the multi-million dollar vineyard business.

Pressing my foot on the clutch of my Honda, which I barely reached with the seat this far back and the steering wheel rubbing along my tummy, the tears fell freely. Life was already complicated, and this surprise in my belly just added to it.

"Hey, little one. I promise I'll do right by you. Mommy's just having a moment." Relief settled in with a gentle motion traveling across my belly. "That's right. I'll keep you safe, and you and I can conquer the world."

One turn of the key and the tires ate up the road for the half-hour drive south back home to wait out the event that was soon to change life one more time in the last ten months.

***

"Mom, don't cry." My feet sat on the coffee table, and a large bowl of ice cream rested on the alien.

"I wanted to be there to help you. Your dad just can't manage the vineyard here alone; I mean, not with his bad shoulder, and Sanchez gone for two more weeks."

My fingers trembled with anger and frustration. She wasn't pleased when I called her back in March with the news. She and my dad still shook their heads when I called in December, letting them know Charles and I broke it off—more like I broke it off, and he spent a few months begging forgiveness. *Bastard*. He knew nothing of love and commitment.

The "baby call" knocked them off the grapevines when the words, "Surprise, I know how Mary did it!" came floating out of my mouth with no explanation of the father. *Strained*—that's how this entire pregnancy unfolded.

"It's okay, Mom. You know I'm gonna need help when I get back to work." Another thorn in her side, as she lived under the rock that women with children stayed home; hence, why Charles fit the bill for them. He would take care of me, and I could pop babies out and be Susie homemaker.

"Keep us posted. We'll figure something out."

"Will do. Keep the phone line open. The next call should be all about the alien!" My fingers sifted through Sadie's neck hair as she rested her chin on what was left of my lap.

"Love you. You know you can—"

Irritation tensed my muscles, and I muttered, "I can handle this without help. I'm fine here in Oregon. I love my job. Love you. Talk to you soon." I clenched my fist as I slammed the receiver down, unsure about how to handle the whole truth of my situation. However, growing up on the outskirts of Napa in the wine country, I learned what I didn't want for myself. I didn't want things handed to me. The preschool job I earned on my own merit. Nobody handed me my degree in early childhood behavior. Nobody went back and finished my teaching credential for me. Nobody hung that silver spoon over my head and gifted me anything. I earned every bit of what I had. And this new baby was mine too. All mine. I earned it, too. *Well*, I certainly helped facilitate its creation.

"Sadie, you and I can raise the alien, right?" She lifted her head and wagged her nub.

"The three of us will make this right. Like the musketeers, only I guess I'm the one who can make decisions." I placed my hands on the back of the couch and huffed out as I lifted off the cushion.

"This waddle better go away after all this," I grumbled to myself as Sadie turned circles around me. "That's right, Sadie, you keep all those Aussie herding skills sharp. We're going to need them." I chuckled to myself, knowing if someone were listening to me, they'd assume I was an old shrew with only dogs as my friends or commit me to Bedlam.

Sadie lay on the floor, chewing a bone while I settled back onto the couch with the ice cream carton. It's too much energy to scoop it into a bowl.

The doorbell buzzed in time with the frustrated bite sliding down my throat. "Shit, I need to stand up, sweet bug." I gurgled down the vanilla and rubbed the belly. A strange warmth trailed down my leg when I stood.

I groaned in frustration. "Great! And now we're peeing on ourselves, baby alien. Oh, Sadie, this is pathetic."

The girls greeted me on the other side of the door, and immediately, all three stared at my wet pants. "Hey, I'll be right back. Apparently, I needed to use the bathroom, and standing up caused an issue."

"You sure that's pee?" Melody bent closer. "It has the same odor my mom had when her water broke, and I drove her to the hospital when I was sixteen. And look at Sadie." She points where Sadie now paced back and forth right behind me.

"She's fine. She's been glued to me since I got home."

Julie wrapped an arm over Melody's shoulder. "Dogs know things."

"I don't know. I've been uncomfortable so damn long, I can't decide what's what. Let me go pee."

"You're never walking right again." Shelley grimaced as Dr. Ashton cut the umbilical cord.

Dr. Ashton gave the baby a quick volley in her hands. "He's a big boy for sure."

"Boy?" My heart stopped momentarily.

"Boy." Dr. Ashton laid him on my chest, and one of the nurses brought a warm blanket over him and rubbed his back until he fussed. "Time of birth: two-forty-five am

Calculation

on October first." One nurse jotted down notes and turned on the warming table.

A tear slipped down onto his head, and relief of his safe arrival washed over me. All the hard work for the last nine months wrapped up tight on my chest. He wasn't covered in the baby goo I saw on the birthing film, and his head looked as if he belonged in the Saturday Night Live skit for the Conehead family.

The nurse leaned over the bed, rubbing his back while noticing my panic. "Don't worry, his head will reform. He had a tight fit." The girls giggled in the background, but it all faded away when the dirty blond-haired baby and I stared at one another for what felt like an eternity. His blue eyes a reminder of the man I spent a few dates with—this boy his spitting image. The last time I saw those eyes New Year's Eve in the throes of passion. The next morning I slipped out of the hotel room in Portland—the last time I'd been to Portland. Little did I know my innocent rebound tryst would end in this moment of pure joy—and me celebrating a new life alone.

"I need to get this big guy weighed and measured." The nurse gathered him up, and the cold replacing his warm body turned the faucet of my tears on harder.

"Don't worry. She's only going two steps from the bed to do all his tests." Dr. Ashton pulled on something and asked me to push.

"Oh Lord, what is that?" Julie gagged a little.

The chuckle from Dr. Ashton brought me back to reality. "The placenta, and it's a healthy one. He had a great deal going on in there. Good news, only a minor tear to repair. You did great, Ximena."

I whispered through the tears, "Thank you." Deep down, my friends were all novices at this birth stuff too, and now we all stared at the little prince on the warmer.

"He's perfect. Nine pounds, ten ounces." The nurse reached in her pocket for a measuring tape. "Perfect head, great chest, and this little man is long. Twenty-two inches. No wonder you couldn't breathe."

I sniffed back the wave of awe, and the highlights of the last few months flooded me.

"Do you know how big the father was at birth or any history? This is all extremely important stuff to know, Ximena." My *mother frowned at me during Easter when I visited.*

"Mom. I can do this. I'll be fine. Have a little faith."

"For God's sake, do you even know his birthday?" She tapped her hands on the counter and stared out the kitchen window.

"I think—"

"You think? What were you thinking? I love you, but a child is a huge responsibility, and I knew you were up to

Calculation

things living in Oregon. I just never figured it would be—" her hands wave around aimlessly. "This." her eyes fell to my still tight flat stomach.

"Maya, let the girl breathe." My father had been silent over the phone in March and spoken little when I arrived home for spring break. He came from a long line of wealth associated with the viticulture and, of course, our own family winery. He met my mother when he spent a semester abroad in Spain. I never guessed he'd be the logical one with my news.

"John, be serious. She doesn't want our help. How is she going to raise this child on her measly salary?

"I have faith in Ximena. She knows we're all here for her."

Finding strength in my voice, I uttered, "He's an Aquarius."

My father wrapped my hands in his as my mother turned from the sink and cocked her head. "You know his sign? Is that going to bring in child support?"

"Stop. I'm not going to tell him. This is my problem, and I'll handle it." With a tight squeeze to my father's hand, my feet marched me out of their kitchen, and I cried myself to sleep that day. That became the last time I named my baby a "problem." The last time I viewed my situation as anything other than a sign of good things to come.

Then there was Lorna. "When school starts back in the fall, you will be near maternity leave."

"I understand. But I can do my job. And this year is the year I see myself bonding with the kids better. I'll relate."

She tapped her fingers on her desk. "I have no problem, but if you can't do the job, you go out on maternity leave."

"Thanks. I won't disappoint you."

"I never thought you would. I just don't want your preschoolers having a sex ed day."

When my fingers turned the knob on her office door, I turned back to Lorna. "You know I appreciate your understanding and professionalism."

A warm smile adorned her face. "You're like the daughter I never had. I also know if anybody can do this, you can. Just make sure you're doing what's right for the baby."

"I promise."

Lorna kept her professional decorum facade together outside of the four walls of her office, but her support grounded me in ways I'll never be able to thank her.

"Ximena, you all right?" Shelley held my hand, and the room of women all quieted and stared at me.

"I'm fine. Just overwhelmed."

"Did you decide on a name?" Melody peered over the warmer as the nurse

Calculation

swaddled him before handing him back to me.

"Yeah. I think his name should be Marcus. Marcus Caelum."

AQUARIUS

JANUARY 21ST – FEBRUARY 20TH

AQUARIUS

Chapter Six

Caelum

"Right there, Ethan."

With a blast of air, the truck jerked to a stop in front of Shepherds of the Cloth, our community service event for the year. A private school on the far north end of Portland, I picked this location since it held a special place in my heart.

"Let me go check in, and I'll be right back." I swung the heavy steel door open and hopped out, my boots a heavy *thump thump* on the asphalt. Memories circled around me, my life reverting back to my childhood days as I pushed through the office doors.

"Hi, Caelum." Mrs. Barlow, as her nameplate declared and a permanent fixture in the office since I could remember, circled around her desk and pulled me close. She remembered every child, big or small, that ever attended Shepherds. Quite a feat over her thirty-year career.

"Hey, Mrs. B. How are you?"

With a squeeze, she pulled away. "I'm great. Mr. Barlow retired this year, and I'm thinking about it, too—next year." A frown passed over her face as she gazed at decades of framed pictures hanging on the wall from past graduating classes. "I'll miss it."

"I'm sure you will. Everyone depends on you to keep them running like a well-oiled machine. I'm not sure anyone could replace you." The radio on my hip squawked as the door to the principal's office opened.

A slim woman wearing a forest-green tailored suit stepped out into the front office. Bright gray eyes shone behind a pair of trendy glasses as she enveloped me in a hug. Years of racquetball kept her fit and strong, something she needed in her position.

"Hey, Lorna." I held on to the woman I knew my entire life. A sorority sister and best friend of my mother's from college, and a steady guest at our home growing up. I respected her and looked up to her as a surrogate parent.

"Caelum, I will never get over how tall you got. Good grief. I need a step ladder to get my arms around you." A happy glow lit her face as she let me go. "Thanks for coming today. The children are very excited to see the fire truck."

I followed Lorna as she swept back into her office and surveyed the front of the school through her office window. "I'm happy to be here. I know I felt the same way when I was their age."

Calculation

"Indeed. It appears our parents are also excited."

Minivans filled with soccer moms and their kids pulled into the drop off lane in front of the office. Their eyes focused on my crew standing by the truck and less on their little monsters bolting to the sidewalk. "You might want to direct traffic out there. The moms are causing a bit of a traffic jam." I snickered and flipped the chair around in front of her desk so my uniform didn't catch on anything.

Lorna shook her head and tsked. "You boys. I swear I can't take you anywhere." The twinkle in her eye as she watched the mothers rubber neck and forget their purpose let me know the boys put on a good dog and pony show for everyone out there.

"Caelum, I realize it's warmer today than the last several weeks. Could they maybe put their shirts back on? This is a school you know. We aren't taking photos for the charity calendar."

"What?" I jumped over the chair for a better view, ready to beat my crew's ass. I gave them strict instructions. Smile and wave *only*. Ethan, Paul, and Ash smiled and waved to the kids as they walked by. Some of the children stood along the fence, enraptured by the flashing lights and large red metal truck; their mouths slack and backpacks forgotten. From where I stood, all three appeared fully clothed and models of upstanding public servants. "Lorna," I growled. "You're lucky my mom is your best friend. Fu--. Uh, you almost gave me a coronary." A twist of her head with an arched eyebrow at my almost slip of the F-bomb had me back in eighth-grade detention hall writing sentences until my fingers cramped and stopped working. "I think I'll go scout out the breezeway and start setting up."

A hand landed on my arm as she pointed with the other to a rounded wooden paddle with drilled holes mounted in a shadow box on her wall. Scrawled signatures covered its surface in a rainbow of permanent colored markers. "I believe your name is on there somewhere, right?"

"Yep." I nodded. She knew damn well my name was on there. Known as 'The Great Redeemer,' the paddle, along with a significant group of women in Portland, was intimately acquainted with my ass.

"Watch your mouth around the kids." She opened the door and shooed me out. I expected a phone call from my mother later when I got back to the station. Grown and out of the house for years, she still had the ability to make me feel like a dumb kid.

"I'll meet you shortly. And Caelum?"

"Yes?" I paused. Something in her tone held me at the threshold of her office.

Calculation

"No shenanigans, or I'll tell your crew about the summer you went skinny dipping in the pond full of leeches."

I'm going to kill my mother.

"Yes, ma'am. I'll be on my best behavior." I slinked away from her office like I did fifteen years ago, suitably chastised and dreading facing my parents when I got home.

Ash, Paul, and I leaned against the truck and waited for the bell as Ethan changed into his costume. All about the same height and build, cocky grins spread over our faces as the three of us garnered stares from the ladies supervising the playground. I tipped my head at a group hovering together on the periphery. They gave a tentative wave and ducked close like conspirators. One pointed at us for a brief moment, right before her friends pulled her away to another part of the playground.

"Fucking, Ethan."

Paul gave a laugh as Ethan weaved his way over from the main building. Dressed in a big black and white polka dot dog costume, he made a point of hugging every woman he passed with exaggerated enthusiasm. Giggles followed in his wake as he 'licked' their faces before moving to the next victim.

On the opposite side, a hoard of children moved over the playground like locust over a wheat field. They flitted about for brief moments in time before descending on another toy. Ping ponging back and forth, their energy was boundless and carefree. A woman with sable colored hair pulled back into a ponytail caught my eye. She paced along the edge of the jungle gym, monitoring the smaller children as they hung from the monkey bars. The confident way she carried herself familiar in some way I recognized, yet I questioned why.

"You know, Cap. They are ripe for the picking over there." Ethan strolled up in his ridiculous outfit, pointing to the trail of broken hearts in his wake. His conquests followed him with their eyes as I rolled mine in exasperation.

"Dude, you're almost as bad as Cap. Panties combust when he does shit like that." Ash knocked Ethan on the shoulder as he waved toward the playground again.

"Nah, Cap doesn't roll like that anymore. The pretty girl from the bar last Christmas got under his skin." Ethan twirled around and moon-walked back and forth as two heads swiveled my way.

"What?" My question came out a little more defensive than I wanted. My engineer knew too

Calculation

much. Saw too much. Understood more than any young person in his position should. He'd nailed me down in the first thirty seconds after I sat on his interview board a few years ago. We started with the basic 'get to know you' questions, then moved to what HR wanted us to spit out. I asked Ethan, "How do you respond to distraction in the workplace?" He turned his twenty-year-old smirk my way, gave me a quick once over, and answered, "There are no distractions. Only the plan and execution of the job at hand. Anything else is irrelevant." *Apparently, my reputation precedes me. No nonsense and straight shooter. Strong character. I need this kid.* I moved heaven and earth for his assignment to my crew once his promotion to engineer took place.

"Listen, it's not like that. I'm going through a dry spell right now." With arms crossed over my chest, I glared at my nosey crew. Damn Ethan and his big mouth.

"You lied to us?" Ash grabbed Ethan and yanked him back to where I stood under the firing squad. "You weren't really working on the house with Jordan? You were sulking at home while we went out clubbing without you?"

Obviously, the daggers I stared at my crew missed because they all laughed. Even Ethan, in the fucking dog suit.

"Cap, it's okay you're whipped. We still like you." Paul snorted and bent over laughing as I glowered next to him. Sure, make fun of me now. Wait until you bastards fall. I'll clap at the horror of realization upon your faces and watch your demise with a bottle of beer and popcorn.

Ethan held a fur-covered hand out in front of me as his body shook under the costume.

"What?"

Paul laughed harder as Ash joined in the fun next to him.

"I'm afraid I need your man card, Cap." Ethan stared at me through the eye slits of the damn costume. The way his eyes creased at the side, I guessed a shit-eating grin split his mouth wide; I wanted to pound it right off.

"Fuck you. All of you."

The recess bell *clange*d in the distance as I flipped off my crew. I wasn't whipped. It was a dry spell. Tomorrow, after I got off shift, I'd take the guys out and show them how things really were. *Maybe.*

"Okay, Cap. I think we're ready." Lights flashed from each corner of the truck as Paul and Ash put the finishing touches on the tables. Each one overflowed with crayons, coloring books, posters of Sparky the Dog, and official Junior firefighter badges each child could take home with them. Ethan strolled around, dressed in the official Sparky dalmatian costume waving at

Calculation

the kids through their classroom windows and hugging any stray female roaming outside the breezeway gates. An icon of fire departments everywhere, Sparky was an instrumental part of early education and fire safety at home. Our visit today provided reminders to the children and adults about what to do in case of an emergency.

"As soon as the bell rings, the students will start making their way to the side where the different colored blankets are laid out. Once we finish the education piece, each class will take turns at the tables, then follow their teacher back through the gate." I peered out over the lines of children headed our way. Their energy alight in the way they wiggled in line, their teachers using the whip of their voice to steer them ahead.

To think, all of us, during some part of our life, did the same thing. Here I was making sure that tradition continued. I hoped someone gained inspiration in our work and wanted to do the same thing when they were adults.

Several classes weaved around the truck and sat on their designated blanket. A final class filled out. The smallest of the bunch arrived last, with the pony-tailed woman parting ways and Lorna settling them. They sat in the front, eyes wide in their faces, and mute with wonder.

"Shut it!" I grumbled at Ash and Paul as they bickered behind me about something I couldn't hear over the chatter of excited voices. Whatever it was needed to wait.

Lorna introduced us, and I took the reins. Of course, Sparky, a.k.a. Ethan, was a big hit. The kids cheered when he did the right thing and booed when he did the wrong thing during our safety quiz. An industrious mother showed up with her camera and offered to take pictures of the classes with Sparky and the truck. I slipped around the front with Paul and Ash as we waited for the chaos to die down.

"I get to be Sparky next year," Paul mumbled as Ethan posed for another picture between two different women.

"I'm betting we'll need a new costume next year. He's getting more action in that than his uniform. Don't be surprised if he takes it home with him." Ash rolled his eyes and leaned against the passenger side door as Lorna rounded the truck.

"Thank you so much for coming. The children are beside themselves." A junior firefighter sticker decorated her lapel where I had placed it earlier, making her honorary Captain for the day. "I'm afraid our Christmas pageant this afternoon will be quite tame after Sparky."

Lorna leaned back and called out, "Miss De Luca, come meet my friend. Well, more my son than a friend."

Calculation

A woman that starred prominently in my dreams and dressed far more conservatively than the last time I saw her, pony-tail and all, rounded the cab behind Lorna and skidded to a stop. A grin split my face. One so wide, even the damn cat in Alice in Wonderland couldn't beat it. With a smack of my lips, I stuck my hand out and practically sang her name like the Hallelujah chorus. "Miss De Luca, how nice to meet you. I'm Captain Ranald, Caelum Ranald." I held her hand much longer than polite as I drank her in. A little softer around the edges and sporting a boob job she couldn't hide under the jacket and apron she wore.

I heard a smack, and Ash crowed behind me, "You owe me a hundred bucks. I *told* you it was her. The one who tamed Cap."

No fucking way. She's been here with Lorna the whole time? I shoved my hands inside the pockets of my turnouts. Refusal to show weakness paramount during this impromptu reunion. The guys snickered behind me and yelled to Ethan as I watched an entire movie play out across her face. Regret? Remorse? Fear? Relief? She looked a little green around the gills and wobbled a bit in her shoes. I held back as Lorna jumped in.

"You doing okay, Miss De Luca?"

"Yeah, sorry. I guess I'm more tired than expected."

Tired my ass. I watched the lie leave her lips and circle around before it landed like a lead balloon at her feet. *What's really going on?*

"Caelum, Miss De Luca just became—"

Mina interrupted Lorna with a clipped response. Something I learned a long time ago you didn't do if you wanted to stay on her good side.

"I didn't sleep well, Captain Ranald. Some nights just work that way." She shrugged, looking defeated and uncertain. Something I didn't expect from my previous vibrant and plucky date.

"I understand. Lorna tells me you keep these little folks on their toes. I must say I admire anyone who can harness this kind of energy." I winked and offered her an olive branch.

She cleared her throat, and I watched the muscles in her neck contract as she swallowed several times before finding the words she needed. "Well, it's nice to meet you, and thank you to you and your team?" Her comment came out as a question in my ears, a frown forming on her face as she plowed ahead. "For coming to share with the kids. If you'll excuse me. I need to get them ready for the performance." With a turn of her heel, she walked away from me again and didn't look back.

I vowed this was the last time.

AQUARIUS

AQUARIUS

JANUARY 21ST – FEBRUARY 20TH

Chapter Seven

Ximena

"Tommy, can you please zip up your jacket? We don't want you sick for break."

His big blue eyes blinked slowly as his chubby hands struggled with the task.

"Here." I knelt down and saw the problem. "Hold tight, let me free this material and—" My finger shook while I edged the zipper back down to free the material from the track of the zipper.

"Wow! Mif Duh Wuca, you're good at dat." His open lipped grin shone from ear to ear.

"Next time, let me know, and I'll make sure to help you before it gets too stuck to fix. Now, go join your class line by the door."

I slipped a glove over one hand and grabbed the keys to the classroom. With one pass over the empty chairs and the buzz of energy whispering around the door to the classroom, a sense of warmth flashed over me. The end of my third week back and Marcus was sleeping all day and waiting for me the moment I arrived home. Thank my lucky stars I only signed on for a three day work week this year, knowing the stork delivery would rock my world. *Much like his father did in making him.*

I shook the thought of his father out of my head, wondering why that idea popped into my thoughts. Caelum hadn't been anywhere in my recent memories other than signing a birth certificate with father as unknown. Something I knew I'd be explaining later to my son and expecting the pushback from him when he figured out he was a happy little surprise stowaway.

"You guys ready to meet the firemen and learn all about how the truck works and their job?"

The rowdy cheers and bouncing bodies created an energy that only increased with each step closer to the parking lot as we wound around the playground and out the side fence. Lorna waved her hand at Sasha, who led the class, skipping each step of the way. It took me some time to realize how much I truly enjoyed teaching three-year-olds with all of their honesty and innocence. A little life lesson I learned after having my own son.

"Miss De Luca, how you holding up after your first three weeks back in the saddle?" Lorna patted my shoulder as I passed by her, trailing the twelve busy bodies toward the red fire truck.

"I'm good. Baby is sleeping a little more. I swear he waits until I get home and then nurses until the early dawn so he can skip using a bottle, though."

She chuckled, keeping her pace next to mine. "They sometimes switch their hours. He'll figure it out."

Four other classes circled the truck, and their teachers looked like ranch hands working on getting them seated on the blankets laid before the truck. Several firefighters stood in yellow suits; I think they called it turn out gear, but fire vernacular was not my language.

As my sweet cherubs nestled into place on their blankets, I stood behind them, noting one of the men looked vaguely familiar. He stared at me with his boyish good looks, but then again, it might have been my sleep-deprived self, begging for a little attention from a male older than newborn or three.

"Lorna, can you watch them a few minutes? I need to use the restroom."

"I got 'em." She nodded as I turned and walked back to the building.

"Shit." My milk let down as the warm water touched my hands. "Good going forgetting the nursing pads." I cursed myself and grabbed my painting apron to shield my jacket from leaking through. My mother's tirade of disappointment yammered in my head as I walked back to the kids. She sent me money for a nanny, which I didn't refuse. But her parting comments only brought back the nausea of trying to break away from the De Luca stereotype and making a life of own.

"You know, you can stay at home if you come home and raise that baby right." Her venom kept on for weeks after Marcus arrived. She came to visit for two whole weeks, well she intended on staying longer, which almost sent me straight to the psych ward.

"You're burping him wrong." She grabbed him out of my arms to demonstrate.

With a disappointed glare at my freezer, she noted, "He's going to need more milk stashed at home if you plan to leave his fragile self with a stranger."

The kicker to it all came at two in the morning the third week we settled into a pattern. She barged into my room with fear coating her from head to toe. "Don't lay him in your bed when you nurse. He'll smother."

My father rushed in, turning at the sight of my breast flopping about as Marcus cried over the disturbance. The reality of the situation forced my father's hand into becoming the arbitrator of our heightened tension. He did settle the nanny issue by providing me a monthly check for help; relief washed over me when he left it to me to choose who would come to help with

Calculation

Marcus. My mother frowned when he took control, but it helped settle us.

When he packed my mother up to leave, the following morning, he kissed me goodbye and whispered in my ear, "She only loves you to the core of her heart. I promise she means well. Give her time. You'll seek her advice, and you'll both be richer for it." I squeezed him tight, speechless because somewhere deep inside, I knew he spoke the truth.

I loved both of my parents dearly, but the legacy of the De Luca vineyard of California, and the beautiful mix of her Spanish heritage, became a thorn in my side. Deep in my soul, I knew my life followed a different path. Something more rich, more pay it forward, more something I wasn't sure of yet but well aware it existed.

Lorna called out to me behind the corner of the cab of the truck as I closed the fence to the playground. "Miss De Luca, come meet my friend. Well, more my son than a friend."

My feet stopped like a petulant child as I rounded the cab of the truck. There stood the man that one year ago I had met in a bar. Dressed in his fire gear with a Cheshire grin plastered from dimple to dimple on each cheek, he licked his lips before addressing me.

His large, calloused hand stretched my direction as he smoothly sang my name,

"Miss De Luca, how nice to meet you. I'm Captain Ranald, Caelum Ranald." A flame flickered in his eyes, and he held my hand a little too long.

One of the guys, the one I thought was familiar, high fived the man to his left and chuckled under his breath, "You owe me a hundred dollar bill. I told you it was her. The one who tamed Cap."

A lump sat heavy in my throat. My knees wobbled a touch. The Devil, sitting front row on my shoulder, tapped his finger against his lips. Pain seared hot and fast as he glared at my never to be seen again one-night, well, two-night stand. The angel on the other side sighed in relief as if Cupid arrived to make my mother happy.

"You doing okay, Miss De Luca?" Lorna interrupted the mild anxiety attack whiplashing inside my flustered head.

"Yeah, sorry. I guess I'm more tired than expected."

"Caelum, Miss De Luca just became—"

I hushed her in a panic. "I just didn't sleep well, Captain Ranald. Some nights just work that way." I shrugged, cringing inside at the awkwardness spilling out around me.

"I understand. Lorna tells me you keep these little folks on their toes. I must say I admire anyone who can harness this kind of energy." He winked my direction and waited for me to speak.

Calculation

I cleared my throat, but the lump refused to budge. "Well, it's nice to meet you, and thank you to you and your team?" It came out as a question. "For coming to share with the kids. If you'll excuse me. I need to get them ready for the performance."

"Oh, my God. That was him, wasn't it?" Shelley hovered around me as I entered back through the gate with the kids playing on the playground for fifteen minutes before we shuffled them into their costumes and finished out the last day of school before break.

Julie waltzed over with her know-it-all attitude on full display. "Well? Now what, MILF." Melody provided no help as she waited with her hands on her hips for my response.

"I'm not doing anything. He'll drive away, and everything goes back to the status quo."

"Are we taking bets on that? Because I have money on him. With that look he gave you, you're far from done in his eyes."

∼∼∼
∼∼∼

The third day of vacation and the girls begged me to join them at the pub. I refused the invitation for our annual end of season stomp back to Portland on Friday.

However, my nanny was ready to kick me out, and I agreed to join them.

In the last two months, with the arrival of Marcus, my new life sent me home to relieve Margo, my nanny. A retired woman who lived two houses down and did child care for a living. She offered to watch Marcus when she realized being home alone after her husband passed away six months ago wasn't how she envisioned her retirement. The beautiful part about Margo was, she allowed me time to go to the gym and grocery shop without toting Marcus everywhere. A win-win for getting my body back in shape, all except for the nursing boobs. They were now a nice full C when full of milk, something I never knew I didn't want, and I prayed they'd shrink back once he and I decided it was time to give up our food train together.

Shelley picked me up at noon. It gave Margo a chance to sleep in, and I figured the bar might not be too busy on a Monday afternoon, right?

"You bitch!" Shelley screeched when I opened the car door. "How are you like nine weeks post-Marcus, and your jeans fit better than before?"

Heat rose up my neck. I thought the same thing when I passed by the mirror in my room. "Lucky, I guess."

Calculation

"I guess, too. Now, if you only had on a shirt to show off those boobs!" She cackled as she pulled away from the curb.

"Stop. Those need to go. When Marcus finishes using them up, I want to wear my button-up tops again. Right now, I can't quite button them. It looks like the button is getting strangled." The laughs settled into silence as we continued on the annual excursion.

"So when are you headed home?" Julie threw out to no one particular as she sat in the back seat with her arm around Melody. They shared a love most people never found.

"Break is early this year. I mean, Christmas isn't until Friday. Are we going to your parents first or mine?" Melody shifted in her seat. Julie's parents loved them both, but Melody's still claimed she was going through a phase.

"Well, I'm headed to my folks tomorrow afternoon until New Year's day." Shelley glanced at me in the passenger seat as she turned the car into the parking lot behind The Eye of the Tiger.

"My dad is sending the company jet to the airport on Wednesday. I might fib and say Marcus is sick and can't fly. I'm not ready for everything back home."

Shelley's hand rubbed against my knee. "I forgot. Charles is back in Napa, isn't he?"

"Apparently he took on a few clients who needed investor help, and he's been the liaison between Wall Street and those small wineries. I don't need him and his secretary looking down on Marcus and me."

A group "Ah" echoed in the car as we all opened our doors and stepped toward the pub. I slowed before the door. Hesitant, as a year ago, the entrance to The Eye forever changed my life. A life that forced me to own my choices and showed me how much I do like my career decision and my son—*the best gift of all.*

Julie pulled me in the door with the welcoming commentary, "Come on. You can get yourself a lemonade and drive all of us drunk girls home."

"Perhaps next year, it will be one of you pregnant or nursing." We slid into a booth instead of sitting at the empty bar. The tradition of sitting in the third booth from the dance floor kept on despite the section not being lit like the ones closer to the bar.

With all the college kids away, Monday afternoons were not tremendous bar dancing opportunities. We held ourselves true and played the jukebox, they drank, and we shared a few pub specials of potato skins, onion rings, and jalapeno poppers. I refrained since Marcus might not handle spicy well.

The theme song played as the clock struck three. I turned my attention to the

Calculation

barback change over as Brad, the owner, wiped it down with his eyes focused on our table.

With a sigh, I suggested, "You guys ready to go?" Brad's stare sent a chilly reminder to me. He and Caelum were good friends, and my time was up.

"Oh, come on. We haven't had our traditional dance to *We Are Family,* and I'm not drunk yet." Shelley sipped the rest of her margarita and signaled for another.

Julie and Melody slipped from the booth with a handful of quarters ignoring me. Everything inside me prayed for them to follow my lead and leave. But nothing aligned in my universe as the door opened and in waltzed Caelum, holding the door open for a woman with a double stroller. I watched with envy as he guided her to a room off the other side of the bar. To my dismay or delight, I couldn't decide which, my gaze lingered on a mirror that reflected their actions. He helped her unlatch each child and place them in high chairs. The infants were noodles in the seats but tried to right themselves. She glowed with her eyes on the children, each sitting on either side of her. Caelum played with the finger of one as the baby held onto his hand. The stabbing pains in my chest arrived in waves with each tender act they shared with the children. The movie played out in slow motion as others began joining Caelum's family in the private room.

My palms sweated, my head spun, and my heart cracked in two on the spot. I wrestled myself out of the booth and ran to the restroom, locking the door behind me.

The crystal knob for the cold water refused to budge at the first sink. Rapid breaths overtook me as anxiety pumped through my veins. *The fucker had been married.* No wonder he was fine with two nights of sex only. How could I be so stupid? From Charles to him. Pushing off the first sink, I slid over to the second, where the faucet worked fine. Cupping my shaking hands under the stream, I gathered the water and splashed it down my face. Looking up to the mirror, I noted the bags hanging heavy under my eyes. Twenty-four was not my finest year. Blinking twice, I moved myself to the paper towel dispenser and pulled quickly, while water dripped from my face. The rough paper towel scraped my cheeks as I dried the water and regained control. Time passed me over. The girls were either packing themselves in the car or finding another way back home. I glanced again at myself and begged God for a clear path out of the pub.

Unfortunately, my bad decision smirked at me from the wall adjacent to the restroom door. His plaid flannel shirt clung to him, and his forearms mocked me as they peeped out from below where he had rolled his shirt. His jean-clad legs crossed at the ankle; he appeared under control and held time in his hands.

"Well, hello again. It must be that time of year."

My hands found my hips, and I gained my strength, knowing he had a wife in the other room and blatantly disregarded her commitment to him and vice versa. Full steam ahead, I pressed the issue. "Well, isn't this sweet. You settle your wife and kids and come back here to what, fuck me—"

The lock to the men's room snicked, and a handsome man with coffee-brown hair and a superman curl walked out with his head down, checking his fly. "Hey. Caelum, thanks for helping with Bartlett and the kids. This holiday party is going to be the best." He lifted his chin and froze.

"Miss De Luca." He lingered on the a. "This is my best friend, Jordan. And Jordan, this is Miss De Luca. I know her as Mina. Not sure what her real name is." He raised a brow and uncrossed his arms.

Humble pie tasted terrible. I swallowed hard and extended a hand. "I'm Ximena De Luca. Nice to meet you, Jordan."

He stuttered, "Yo—You're the one! Caelum. Ximena. Nice to meet you, but I have my own business to attend to." And with a wide grin and double tap on

Maggie Jane Schuler and Morgan Heyward

Caelum's chest, he left us in the bathroom
hallway—me with my foot in my mouth.

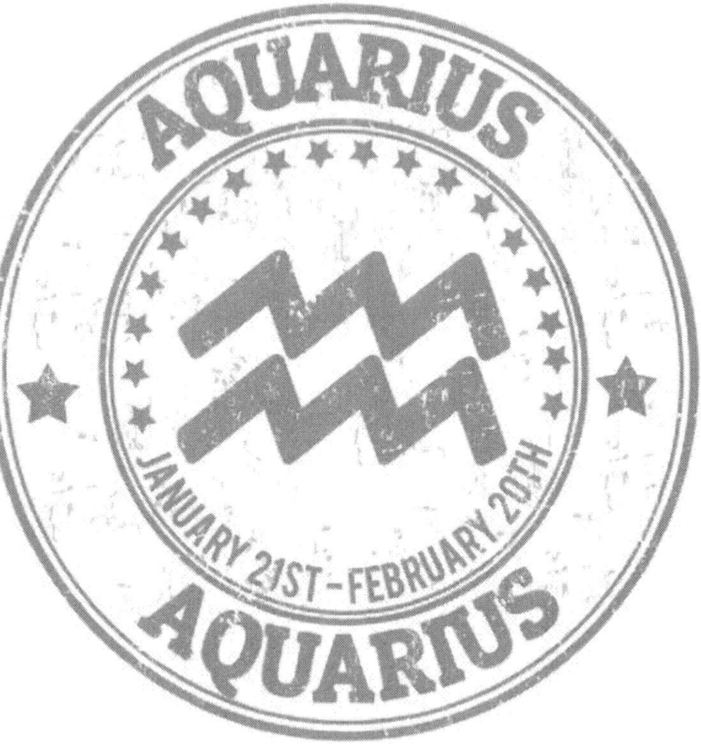
AQUARIUS
JANUARY 21ST – FEBRUARY 20TH
AQUARIUS

Chapter Eight

Caelum

How I wanted to kiss the flushed skin high on her cheeks and the tips of her ears. Her reflection in the mirror as she stomped by the bar caught me off guard. Almost deja vu, since a year to the day, I met her in the very same place. "So, Ximena De Luca, formerly Mina. As in De Luca wines? Or is that a coincidence?"

She sighed, and her shoulders dropped as she muttered, "One in the same."

"Interesting."

The subtleness in her avoidance of the wine caught my attention on New Year's Eve, but when Lorna introduced us, it all came to me so clearly. I read the news and saw the hype that the heiress of the wine country had split with her longtime beau, but none of the pictures showed her; they showed the winery.

"Why?" She shrugged.

"I thought it odd when you turned away from the wine and champagne in our hotel room. It all made sense when Lorna introduced us. Anything more I should know?"

"Nope."

My need to touch her won out over my warring restraint to not push her. I pulled her to me in the quiet of the hallway, where only the music and muffled laughter from the bar drifted in waves as she reluctantly wrapped her own arms around me. Time stood still, and the calculations of what I planned to do if I ever saw her again faded away as she trembled in my hold.

I knew if anyone could break through her nerves and make this situation unfold in my favor, it was Bartlett. She'd been on my ass for months to ask Brad who the mystery girl was, but I refused to ask. More than once, Brad beat around the bush seeking confirmation from me and my irritable behavior. He refused any information unless I admitted my desire for more from the woman with soulful eyes who clipped my tomcat behavior. I teetered once or twice on caving in and admitting she occupied my mind, but stubbornness won every time.

The scent of gardenia in her inky black hair took me back to our last night together. I whispered, breaking the white noise of the bar, "How would you like to meet Bartlett and the twins?" The slight dip of her head spurred me forward. I linked our hands and rejoiced in the contact of her skin with mine. Something I missed since I woke alone for the second time after my rendezvous with her.

"I need to let my friends know—" A quick flash of realization across her face and a frown at the main floor had me scrambling for a solution.

"Let's tell them I've got you tonight, okay? Then let's go meet my friends so you can see who all this unnecessary fuss was about. You'll love them." My wagging brows had her hiding a shy grin behind her hand.

She led me to her friends who were already dancing, their liquid courage in full force as they sang *Funky Town,* out of tune, to a small group of spectators.

She stopped us at the edge of the dance floor. "Caelum, I'm their designated driver. I can't leave—"

"I'll get Brad to handle taking them home. Trust me." With a squeeze of my hand, she wandered forward. Her friends stopped in their tracks when they glanced in my direction. One mouthed an "Oh shit!" while the other shouted, "You better tell him," as the song faded out.

Ximena's hand flew up like a stop sign to her friends. She left them on the dance floor, willing to offer them up to be in Brad's care. Without another spoken word but plenty of the secret messages budding in some sort of sign language spoken through their pupils to one another, she turned away. I tilted my head at the girls and turned on my heel with Mina's hand back securely in mine as we crossed over to our private party.

Baby chatter filled the small room as we entered together, my heart filled full with the knowledge of her name given in truth this time. Bartlett looked up from where she stirred a jar filled with green sludge as Skye and Stella gnawed on their fists in anticipation.

"Hey, Bart. I want you to meet someone." I didn't expect the twins to burst into tears, or Bart shortly after them. A minute into my introduction, I managed to destroy the happiest family on the planet.

"Oh, jeez. What happened?" Jordan walked in, holding a pitcher in one hand and bar food in the other. He scooped up the twins and handed them off to me as he pulled Bart in close. "Did mean old Caelum hurt your feelings, babe?"

"Hey, now," I growled, and the twins started snuffling again, sure to scream soon if I said anything else.

Bartlett removed herself from Jordan's protection and hugged Mina. No introduction passed between them. Mina stood stiff with a big question mark hanging over her head.

"I told you, babe, he found her again." Jordan broke the ice, and Bartlett let go of her bear hug on my girl.

Calculation

My girl. My dream. My everything. Something I figured out in one meeting. I knew she was it for me.

Ximena backed away a step as Bartlett let her go, then the twin cuteness of Stella and Skye shined bright in the quiet room containing all the people I cared about most.

"Ma-ma-ma." Stella pointed at Ximena with her stubby finger covered in drool. "Ma-ma."

"No, sweetie, that's ma-ma." Ximena pointed at a startled Bart.

"Da-da-da." Stella patted my chest, and I kissed her fuzzy head. *Someday, baby girl. She only has to say yes.*

Ximena shook her head and pointed to an equally startled Jordan. "That's da-da."

Fat tears filled Stella's eyes, and her little lip trembled. Her brother, not to be outdone, squealed, "Da. Da." His little hand pounded my chest with the force of his conviction as I waited for Ximena to correct him.

A shocked silence filled the room as I turned to a pale Ximena.

Jordan murmured, awe tinting his words, "They spoke. They've never said anything but gibberish before today."

Tears streamed down Ximena's face as she stared at the babies in my arms. "How could they possibly know?"

"Know what?" Bartlett reached for the babbling duo, leaving my arms empty, waiting for Ximena to answer me.

Through her tear-laced lashes, she whispered, "They're right. We are the parents, as of ten weeks ago."

My mouth dropped open with her admission. *What?* Blood rushed in my ears, its tempo drowning out the pregnant pause weighing heavy over us.

"You have a son."

I sat before I fell over; her whispered words akin to shouting in a library at the top of your lungs.

Bart told me one afternoon, as I hung out with her and the twins, she sometimes sensed their emotions. She couldn't explain their *twintuition*, just that they happened randomly. The babies refused to sleep apart, and always touched in their sleep, something they'd done since birth. Her first ultrasound even showed the twins facing each other, their hands matched palm to palm through their amniotic sacs.

"Jordan, why don't you and Bart take the twins home, and I'll take Ximena home." Stella cooed from Bartlett's arms, "Da-da."

"Guess I'm about to find that out, baby girl."

Calculation

The trip to Ximena's filled me with equal parts of excitement and anger. She only gave her address and filled the rest of the time with silence or an occasional sniff. Why didn't she tell me? This looped in my head over and over. I told her the story about the bar. She knew Brad was a friend of mine. Why didn't she reach out through him? Did she want to keep it a secret forever? That angered me the most. A night I considered one of the best and most emotionally intense of my life, yet one of the most irresponsible, that ended with me waking up alone and Ximena going home with something of mine. Something she kept from me until fate stepped in and called in her marker. Her marker being me. Rather than dishing out my anger, I kept it close to the vest. That's how much she meant to me.

"Turn left at the next stop sign."

"Will do."

A running ticker tape clouded my vision as a highlighted version of the last year drummed through the stagnant silence between us. I visited Brad's bar every Saturday, hoping she'd arrive. In my wildest version, I'd whisk her away and keep her locked in my house until she came to her senses and stayed on her own. Each Saturday, I went home to my empty place, broken just a little more, until I resolved myself to stop looking. One week later, she walked back into my life, in the least likely of places, as an employee of one of my mother's oldest friends.

Fate? Luck? No idea. I wasn't knocking that nor the twins' weird intuition. The whole situation screamed preordained by the gods. Just like one of those old Greek myths I read in college. No way was I knocking a gift horse in the mouth. My horoscope in this morning's paper mentioned my Aquarius nature would solve a problem today and find a love greater than oneself—*definitely fate.*

"No way." As I turned onto her street, a strange recognition greeted me. More mature now, the trees towered over the rooftops. Rooftops of houses I helped build over ten years ago.

"What's wrong?" Present and in the moment, she sat up and looked out the windshield.

"Nothing. Just reminiscing. I helped build this neighborhood when I first started out in construction."

"Really?"

"Really. My first job out of high school. I started as a grunt and earned enough money for a car. Saved me riding the city bus to school."

She patted the leather seats I tooled with care. "You've come a long way since then."

I slid my hand over hers and squeezed. "I sure have." Electricity jolted between our palms. Another sign we were destined.

"That's mine over there." She pointed to a house with a small flower bed filled with pruned rose bushes. A welcome sign on the door greeted us as she flipped the lock and stepped inside. "Margo, I'm home."

"I'm in the kitchen."

A bassinet sat on the floor next to a couch, and reality hit me like the heat of an active fire. Black foggy rings narrowed inside my eyes, and I paused with a hand on the wall. My heart raced, sweat beaded on my lip, and lunch threatened to perform a reverse double flip.

"Ximena, I think your friend needs a chair." An older woman with the weight of the world hanging in her eyes held a bundle shaped like a football just as my knees gave out, and I fell flat on my ass.

"Caelum! Are you all right?"

I nodded, even though my stomach straddled the fence. "Yeah. A little off balance is all."

The woman, who I assumed was Margo, scoffed, "Honey, you're doing a whole hell of a lot better than some. Ximena, help the man up and get him to the couch where it's more comfortable."

Ximena threw her shoulder into my armpit. Together we got my uncooperative limbs moving and on to a gingham covered loveseat in her living room. The football landed in my arms with strict instructions to support its head— I froze. My cool levelheadedness flew out the window. No experience prepared me for this moment. No blood test needed. My own eyes peered back at me through the lens of a miniature human being.

"Wait." I panicked. Holding Skye and Stella felt normal, easy. The ill children I treated and transported to the hospital forced me into a position of authority to help and be in control. But this—this was different. I didn't know what to do when something wasn't wrong. This little one wasn't a one-time transport with parents of his own that knew what the cries meant as they held their baby in their arms. From now until forever, I was his father. The panic settled in my chest.

"I don't know what to do."

"You'll be just fine." Ximena sat next to me as I stared at the little face wrapped in the flannel blanket in my arms. Blue eyes framed in light-brown lashes blinked up at me as a pacifier squeaked at an impressive pace. "Caelum, this is Marcus. Your son."

I can honestly count on one hand how many times I've cried in front of a woman. My mother doesn't count. My vision blurred as I smiled down at the little bundle in my arms, the pacifier in his mouth moving at a mile a minute, his perfect skin. I suddenly

Calculation

needed to see all of him. See all of his little fingers and toes, make sure he was whole and hardy. "Can we take the blanket off? Will he be warm enough without it?"

"Of course."

I placed him on my lap and worked the blanket free. Like opening a present, I lifted the layers away one by one until his little body emerged. Tiny socks and mittens decorated with little ducks covered his feet and hands. I slid those free, thankful for the amazing little person now open to my inspection. "He's so tiny. So perfect." I rubbed a finger along his leg, amazed at the texture of his skin. "So soft."

Tears fell freely and soaked the front of my shirt. Never in my life did I want something this much. This wonderful gift, a culmination of the time I spent with the only woman I'd ever loved. The only woman I still loved. The piece of me she handed over, represented the *us* I dreamed of for the last year. The last year that taught me about desire, heartbreak, and the butterfly theory, as Bart called it. She told me that if you care about something, let it go. If it returns to you, it's meant to be. I remember telling her and her theory to go fuck themselves as I returned empty-handed yet again one Saturday night. Now humbled, the woman I pined after sitting next to me, and the life we created in my arms, I believed her.

"I'm leaving. Call me if you need me tomorrow." Margo grabbed a bag and left. As the door shut, Marcus let out a whine and spit the pacifier out, his little hands now shaking fists in the open air.

"Shit, what did I do?" I stared at my angry son in horror.

Ximena leaned over and scooped him into her arms. "Nothing at all. I'm home now, and he thinks I'm an open bar. Give me a few minutes to feed him, and I'll be right back."

My heart stopped for a beat, thinking of her leaving, even if it was for a moment. The idea of Marcus so new, the zipping thoughts in my head yearned to hoard all the firsts I could before I had to go home. A cold chill passed over my veins as everything inside me claimed them with a fierceness beyond explanation. Ximena didn't want to be kept or corralled; however, evident by her choosing to do this her way from the start. I wouldn't force her into a life with me. I learned that the hard way.

In my brief anxiety-riddled moment, my voice pleaded, "Please, can I feed him?" I wiped the moisture from my face as Marcus snorted in Ximena's arms.

"I don't think he'll take a bottle right now."

"Oh." Disappointment bottomed out and burned in my gut. Already I couldn't

Calculation

provide for my son as I should—as I wanted to.

Ximena sat back down and placed Marcus in my lap. I watched in fascination as she unbuttoned her shirt and pulled at a snap on the top edge of her bra. Her right breast slid into sight, and I gasped. *Not boob job!*

Rounded and much fuller than what she had before, I hoped she'd share them with me again. *I'm still a bastard, but only for you.*

"Can you hold him and prop yourself against the armrest? Put one leg here and the other on the floor." I followed her instructions. Marcus shook his hands and wailed as she took him in her arms once I moved and sat down between my legs. With a hiss, she laid back against my chest as Marcus grunted and gulped with contentment. I helped support her arm and curled mine under hers as we both held our son. Something she could've kept private, yet she shared with me.

"Thank you." I drew lazy eights on her arm as Marcus slowed, and his eyes drooped closed. His belly full and held in arms that loved him without end. With a pop, the seal of his lips broke, and Ximena lifted him to her shoulder. Two burps broke the silence as she tapped his back, and he fell back to sleep.

"Can you hand me his blanket?" Wrapped securely once again, she stood, walked over, and placed him in the bassinet, and then she righted her shirt.

My life was complete.

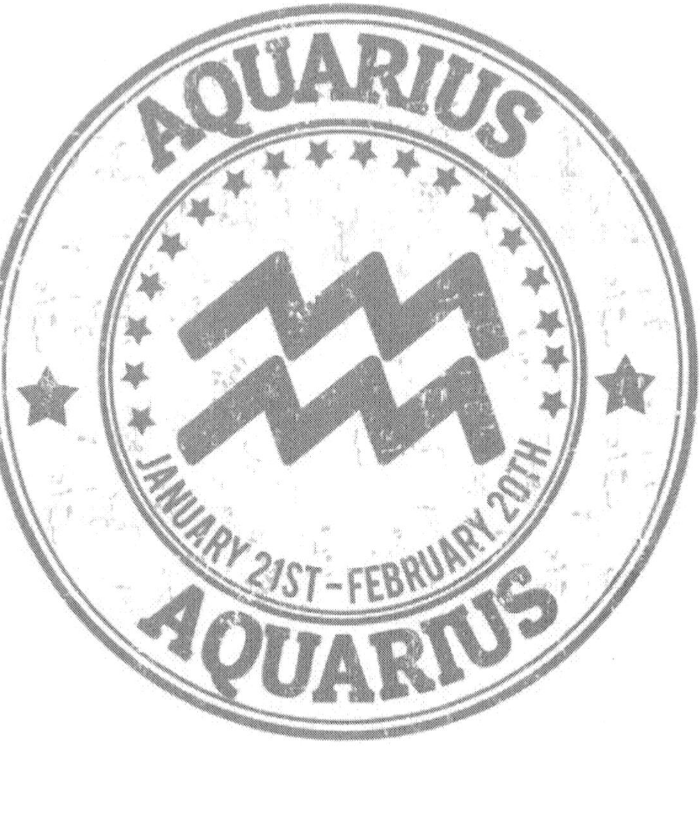
AQUARIUS
JANUARY 21ST-FEBRUARY 20TH
AQUARIUS

Epilogue

Ximena

"Oh, boy, that's a load." Caelum strolled out of Marcus's bedroom with the neck of his t-shirt fitted around his nose, Marcus propped on his hip, and a full diaper and ruined onesie in the other.

My stomach ached as the chuckle rolled through my belly. "You act like it's biohazardous waste every time. How do you even handle your job?"

He closed the back slider and handed Marcus to me. "I don't know what you feed our son, but it isn't right what he can do all the way up his back."

"He's a healthy boy! Are you ready to catch our flight?"

His complexion turned the same ashen gray it had months ago when he saw Marcus for the first time. The thought of meeting my mother and father for the first time kept him a little off his game.

A patterned knock changed his demeanor as he opened the door to Jordan, Bartlett, and the twins. Skylar held one of Bartlett's hands while Stella held tight to the other. Their chubby legs wobbling as they entered my house.

"You guys ready? My dad has the plane landing in about an hour at the municipal airstrip."

"I can't believe we're flying to Napa for a few days. You sure you still want us to come?" Jordan begged the question, knowing Caelum's nerves wore themselves like the noose of the tie he wore on New Year's Eve eighteen months ago.

"I need you there. Her father might kill me." The usually calm Captain Ranald, who faced blazing fires, accidents, and more gruesome sights, paced the floor as rings of sweat formed in the pits of his T-shirt while we waited for the limo service. My mother had been to visit for a few brief moments over the last few months, but I decided to keep Caelum my secret until we figured out how our lives crossed and what we both needed from a relationship. Caelum professed his desires for making Chief of the department, and I expressed how much teaching early childhood education meant to me. He supported my dreams and never once asked about my family's money. Granted, my father already set Marcus up with a trust fund, which I fought him on, but when it came to Marcus, my father held nothing out of reach for his firstborn grandchild.

Calculation

"My mom has a few nannies coming to sit with the kids so we can have some adult time." The black limo pulled to the curb in front of the house as I finished my tidbit of news. Caelum marched back to the bathroom as his breakfast returned.

"As calm as he appears on the job, every time he's faced something big in his life, the captain's exam, our big solar deal, and now you, he can't keep his shit together."

"Eat shit, Jordan." Caelum returned in a new shirt, and his face damp. "I'll be fine."

"We can postpone this if it's—"

"No." Caelum snapped as he picked up our bags. "Our son needs a home with both of us under one roof. You told me it wouldn't happen until we settled things with your parents. I'm done being a visitor and going home at night—alone."

Bartlett dropped her jaw. "I guess he didn't tell you my rules." I shrugged and picked Marcus up from his playmat.

Jordan helped the driver load the bags and, in a not so hushed whisper to Caelum, asked, "Are you kidding me? You've been a fucking monk after all this time?"

I ignored the not so hushed question directed at Caelum.

"She wanted to make sure I was here for the right reasons. I can't blame her. Do you see what happened with my superior swimmers after only two times with her."

"I never thought I'd see the day." Bartlett's comment filtered my direction over her shoulder as she secured the twins inside the limo.

"I told my dad he had to send a limo with three car seats." I buckled Marcus in and handed him his pacifier.

"Not my point. You've really kept yourself from Caelum and not spent a night together?"

"Nope." I popped the p and played with the sleeve of my sweatshirt.

"You realize how much he loves you?" She sat back as Jordan and Caelum settled.

Does he love me? He loves his son for sure. Over the last six months, he abided by my wishes, and we spent time getting to know one another outside of the bedroom. In my situation, with family money, I never experienced anyone who wanted me without the benefits of the family estate lurking in their minds. One of the reasons I refused any discussion about my upbringing and the state of my place within the winery dynasty.

Over the course of the months we spent together, we enjoyed Marcus, fixed his birth certificate, and went about our daily routines without any questions about my family. Bartlett's words rolled over and over while we traveled. Caelum Ranald officially dedicated his hours after work to discovering who I was or am or desired to be.

He never probed me for more than I gave. He never pushed the envelope when I expressed how important our relationship as parents and friends meant in developing a life for Marcus. He never stepped out of line, pushing me for more intimacy. My resolve wavered many times when he'd kiss me hello or goodbye, but our strange beginning, and with Marcus my number one priority, I refused to make a snap decision that impacted my son's future. My chest pounded as the realization of the truth before me hit hard—*he loves me, for me.* A first in my life.

The plane descended into the little Napa municipal airport. Caelum squeezed my hand as I breathed in my new found information. I wanted to drop it all and whisk him away to have my way, but reality took hold: meeting my parents—the priority of this visit—and for the future we sought together.

My mother sat on the porch swing when the limo stopped on the driveway of the mansion I grew up in. She waved as she stood and made her way down the steps to greet us.

"I know where you get your beauty from." Heat rose in my cheeks as Caelum's compliment electrified everything I initially sought in him. That first moment in the pub when we bantered about Coke, and I knew Charles and I were over, he touched my soul.

"You ready?" I fumbled with Marcus's seatbelt, knowing this moment changed our whole world and set the path for our future.

"I've never been more ready!"

"Bullshit," Jordan called out with Skye in his arms, waiting for the limo door to open. "This is the most nervous I've ever seen you. Can we wait, since this might be the last time we ever witness his cocky nature knocked down a few blocks?"

As the door opened, Caelum provided Jordan a solid middle finger salute, all while turning his hips, plastering a toothy smile upon his face, and exiting the car.

"You better stop that right now, or you're being cut off," Bartlett snapped with Stella in her arms.

"Sorry, but he deserves this. Don't you recall his brutal torture when we were dating?"

Bartlett waved a telling finger in his direction as he exited with Skye.

"Get my grandson out of the car," my mother commanded, and all the air in my lungs evacuated because this moment marked the first time I cared about her, or my father, loving the person I planned to spend the rest of my life with.

Calculation

Early dinner with my parents transpired without any issues. Caelum charmed my parents on all fronts. He discussed his job as captain of the fire department. His dreams of becoming fire chief in a few years if he continued blazing his path as he had. Jordan kept my father's interest with talk about the solar power renewable energy he and Caelum developed. Renewable energy excited my dad.

Bartlett and her sweet nature kept my mother entertained. Bartlett, being from California, knew the struggles of the wine culture and wowed my mom with her knowledge of soil, land erosion, and other eco-friendly conversation. I kept silent most of the dinner, listening and praying my parents understood why I loved Oregon. My life resided there with the preschool, my friends, my son's father.

"Let's get these kids bathed, and then we can venture to the tasting room. It's still early." My suggestion brought Bartlett and I out to the guest villas on the north end of the property.

"It's beautiful here." She undressed Stella, while Skye attempted shrugging his own shirt off. His head appeared a little bigger than the hole in the neck.

"Wait until August when it's beastly hot and the crush is almost here. It's not so pretty when it all looks like dead vines. More like a dust bowl until the regrowth season begins."

"I understand why you're in Oregon. I ran from my family for a while, too." She plunked the twins in the bath and waved her hands in my direction to finish undressing Marcus and drop him in with them.

"Really?"

"My older brother never did a damn thing wrong in his life. My parents made sure I knew how wonderful he was. Moving to Oregon and reuniting with Jordan was the best thing to happen to me. I made my transition happen. You have it in you, too."

"Thanks, but I'm the sole heiress to all of this, and I don't want it. The money means nothing to me. My dad works hard and can't leave or won't take my mom on vacation or whatnot. My mom works to keep all the social events together, but I'm not sure how happy this life makes them. I'd rather sell it to my cousins and wash my hands of the whole thing. It's too much loneliness in a sea of expectations."

"I can see that. Your parents are still young. You have time to decide your path, right?"

"Maybe." Squeals and splashes ensued as we slathered the babies in shampoo and

Calculation

soap, before removing them to get ready for bed.

I finished nursing Marcus in my villa as my mother entered. "You almost ready? The sun is going down, and we held the tasting room open for the four of you."

"Shh, he's almost asleep." I rocked him a few more times before setting him the crib. My mother redecorated one of the villas for me at Christmas to give me enough privacy but a beautiful place for Marcus when we came to visit. I appreciated her approach but knew she hoped I'd decide to stay if I felt like I had my own place. Her transparency never overlooked as I knew it was a ploy for my return.

"Caelum is handsome like your son."

"Our son," I corrected for no real reason.

"He's a good man. I like him." My eyes widened at her truthful confession. "I didn't want to like him because I know it only pushes you back to Oregon, but he makes you glow."

"We're figuring things out."

"Don't wait too long; men like him don't stay around indecisive women too long. I'm surprised he's not staying here with you two?" She raised her brow as she refolded a blanket on the couch.

"We're working on things between us."

"I think *you're* working on things. He's a man who knows what he wants. He said so during dinner. Listen more, *Chiquita*, you'll be surprised at what you hear."

My hand shook as I reached for a glass and filled it with water. My mother's words sat heavy. A first in my life where she actually provided advice and didn't express how I created a life outside of her approval. She appeared to understand me. Not who she dreamed I'd become. *My mother saw me, for me, for the first time.*

My startled realization stayed a secret once Caelum waltzed in with Carla and Cielo, my nanny growing up and her daughter. By six, Carla entered Bartlett's villa, and Cielo remained in mine. Both Bartlett and I left our instructions and set out in a golf cart over to the tasting room. My mother and father decided to stay behind in case the kids woke up.

"How did things go with my father after we left?"

Caelum reached for my hand as we entered the large wooden doors adorned with grapevine ornamental ironwork for the handles. "Things went well."

"You're still alive. I'm assuming he's still plotting?" Jordan chuckled from behind us as Bartlett slapped his chest.

A strange calm and calculated expression washed over Caelum. He refused to retort to Jordan, and the lighting in the tasting room dimmed with floating candles flickering over the entire room—the quiet

Calculation

ambiance an eerie mixture of excitement and anticipation. My fingers danced across the wood of the wine barrel holding the ice bucket, the rumpled label of the bottle of De Luca's finest champagne chilled in the middle; the same type Caelum ordered in the hotel room the night we created our miracle.

My heart jumped to my throat at the opening notes of New Edition's *Can You Stand the Rain*.

A tear slipped down my cheek as a whispered, "You remembered," escaped me.

The heat of his chest radiated against the back of me. "Turn around. Look at me, Mina."

With a quick swipe from the back of my hand, drying the tear, I gathered myself and turned. His baby blues created a blaze of warmth that radiated from my chest and pumped through my veins.

"You know I listened to you the whole time. My soul belongs to you, our son, and the future we both dream of. I saved this champagne..." He lifted his head toward the bottle. "...for the right moment after you left me New Year's Day. I waited patiently for fate to bring you back. I plotted every scenario of things I'd do if you returned. What I hadn't calculated was you bringing me all the things I never knew I wanted. I'm telling you this today because with every breath I take, I cannot go on without you. I need you by my side. Ximena, will you be my perfect day and endure the rain, too? Mina, please marry me."

With Caelum down on one knee, nobody breathed as time suspended. In my peripheral, my parents entered with Caelum's mom and dad. I've only met them a few times, and they loved me without judgment. From the shadows, Lorna, Julie, Melody, and Shelley came into the candlelight. Ash, Ethan, Paul, and a few other of Caelum's crew joined us in the tasting room. Surreal—my head spun with the care he placed in making this moment happen.

"You've rendered her speechless. You broke her. Way to go, Cal." Jordan broke my paralysis.

"Yes. Without reservation, yes." I folded into his arms, locked in the knowledge that Caelum Ranald held true in his heart to remain my partner, protector, and love from this day forward.

About the Authors

Maggie Jane Schuler is a wife, mother of three almost-grown children, and teacher by day. While she has always loved to read, the thought of writing her own prose did not strike until she was in the middle of writing her master's thesis. From that point on, she was hooked.

She resides in Southern California. Besides the family and books, she loves baseball. Since the Dodgers, Angels, and Padres are all within a short distance, and the Giants and Athletics a nice weekend jaunt away, she's got plenty of games to take in during the season. Additionally, she enjoys cooking, movies, the beach, and the local mountains. She's most content being with her family engaged in whatever activity they have planned.

Morgan Heyward was raised in the Wild West. Her home state of Arizona subject to intense summer rainstorms, Gila monsters, and the majestic Saguaro cacti. A desert rat through and through, she prefers holing up in the air-conditioned shopping malls during the sweltering summer, rather than braving the snowy Bigfoot populated forests of the Northwest, during the winter. A wife, mother of a teenage human, and cat mom to a clowder of felines, she started her writing journey during NaNoWriMo16, when an author she followed on Facebook, issued the NaNo challenge to all of his fans. That little push three years ago was all she needed to get started. Since that time, she's worked diligently, putting words down and creating a world for those NaNo16 plots and ideas. Her first self-published short story, *A Demon's Miracle*, takes the reader inside for a glimpse of those characters.

When she's not putting words to paper, she's involved in health care and emergency medical services. Raised by a family of nurses, she puts that knowledge to good use toward humans and all of the sick and injured beasties arriving on her front porch. (She's convinced a cat in the neighborhood put up a flyer with her address on it.)

Morgan looks forward to continuing her NaNo journey. She has several projects up her sleeve in the coming year and is always looking for readers and bloggers to share them with.

Also by

Maggie Jane Schuler

THE DIAMOND SERIES
Up To Bat
The Playbook

THE SURF SERIES
In the Surf
Along the Shore

STANDALONES
Resurrection
A Sorcerer's Road to Temperance
Melt Me

Co-Writes
Transformation

Morgan Heyward

STANDALONES
A Demon's Miracle

Co-Writes
Transformation

Made in the USA
Columbia, SC
19 February 2020